Reviews of Graham Garrison's debut novel, *Hero's Tribute*

"The book examines the human condition and succeeds in inspiring readers to follow lives of genuine discipline and faith. Highly recommended."

—CHURCH LIBRARIES

"Fans will appreciate this terrific insightful look at a Hero's Tribute. To be human means to have flaws, but it takes Amazing Grace to move past them to greatness. With a final twist at the eulogy that will leave readers stunned and wanting to join in on the four song tribute, Graham Garrison provides a strong Christian tale."

—MIDWEST BOOK REVIEW

"*Hero's Tribute* is a human drama story and much more."

—BVS REVIEWS

"Mr. Garrison selects an intriguing premise for his debut novel and follows it through with a great narrative style. . . . Excellent story, solidly written and definitely worth the read."

—SUMMIT BOOK REVIEWS

LEGACY ROAD

A Novel

GRAHAM GARRISON

Kregel
Publications

Legacy Road: A Novel
© 2012 by Graham Garrison

Published by Kregel Publications, a division of Kregel, Inc., P.O. Box 2607, Grand Rapids, MI 49501.

Library of Congress Cataloging-in-Publication Data
Garrison, Graham.
Legacy Road / Graham Garrison.
    p.   cm.
I. Title.
PS3607.A7736L44   2012   813'.6—dc23   2011051817

ISBN 978-0-8254-2671-1

Printed in the United States of America

12 13 14 15 16 / 5 4 3 2 1

To my boys, Nicholas and Nolan.
Know that you are loved.

Chapter 1

Wes Watkins took a deep breath and opened the tiny box. Still there. Three months' salary—four if he'd stayed as a small town reporter for the *North Georgia News*. Other than rent, the largest investment of his life, and success hinged on Emmy Stewart saying yes.

Downtown Roswell restaurant noises filtered beneath the men's room door. Wes cradled the box in his hands and studied the ring. The solitaire diamond was sleek and classic—like Emmy.

He remembered vividly the first time he met her, at a Memorial Day barbecue. Lynn Gavin, Emmy's aunt, introduced the pair over ribs and tea, and Wes felt an immediate attraction to Emmy. Wes thought his friendship with Lynn might give him a bit of a leg up on any competition. But he'd had two things going against him. One was that Emmy's blue summer dress and sparkling blue eyes left him wobbling through their conversation like a six-year-old learning to ride a bike without training wheels. And the other, which was more important to Emmy, was that Wes displayed poor rib-eating skills.

"A fork? Really?" were her first words, in a slightly raspy, completely Southern voice. "What kind of self-respecting man eats his ribs with a fork?"

He had fallen in love right there. That had been more than seven months ago. Now it was five hours until the New Year on a Friday night with the whole world opening up for Wes, it seemed. He smiled as he closed the box and tucked it and the memories away. He'd spent too much time in the bathroom already and would hear about it from Emmy.

He took a quick look in the mirror to smooth back his dark hair and smiled to make sure he didn't have something stuck in his teeth. His brown eyes studied his average frame through the reflection. He took in the retreat of his double chin, a little more muscle on his shoulders, his more upright posture—all attributed to Emmy and her active lifestyle.

Then as he pushed through the men's room door, Wes did something that two years ago he would never, ever have done. He prayed, silently thanking God for all the changes in his life.

"What were you doing in there?" Emmy asked. "Powdering your nose?"

Wes laughed. He soaked in her voice, her dimples, her long brunette hair. How had he gotten so lucky? He wasn't sure. Until he'd met Emmy, his disheveled childhood, not much dating in high school and college, and practically no love life in the real world had him thinking he'd be a bachelor forever. He'd reached the midway point of his twenties with no prospects. But then an obituary assignment was handed to him one Monday morning, followed by an unusual request—to also deliver the man's eulogy. The assignment opened the doors to the community of Talking Creek, closed Wes's career as a full-time newspaper reporter, and most importantly, opened his eyes to see beyond his built-in skepticism of people's intentions, to possibly forgive and heal old wounds that'd he buried or tried to ignore. Meeting Emmy only confirmed to Wes he was on the right track.

"Want to join the living?" Emmy said.

Wes grinned and took a bite of chicken parmigiana. "I just wish I could live on this."

Emmy rolled her eyes and let him off the hook. "You should try eating something new. You know I'm going to have you eating tapas yet. I've heard John Smoltz lives around here and *loves* the tapas."

Another plus with Emmy—she was an encyclopedia in all things sports and even gave Wes a run for his money about his beloved Braves.

"Gotta get a better bullpen or we won't have a shot against the Mets," she said between forkfuls of pasta. "Can't depend on the starters all season—not like when we trotted Smoltz, Glavine, and Maddux out there in the 90s. You saw the innings our rotation put up last summer, and it wore them down for the stretch run."

"Do you realize those are some of the most romantic words a man can ever hear?" Wes said. She kicked him under the table.

They finished their dinner and walked to the corner for coffee. "Want to walk through the square before we head down to Atlanta to watch the Peach Drop?" It wasn't a random question, although he tried to play it off that way. He'd planned their route for weeks.

"But it's freezing!" Emmy protested. "And we're watching the Peach Drop from a hotel ballroom, right?"

One of the coldest New Year's Eves of the last few decades, the weatherman had said. And Wes knew Emmy hated being cold. She was a beach girl: tank top and flip-flops complete with sunny skies. The weather was the only part of this day Wes couldn't control, but he wasn't going to wait. He wanted the rest of his life to start right now.

"Come on. I bet a future Hall of Famer like John Smoltz would do it," Wes said, smirking and trying to act cool. "Besides, we never get over here enough to enjoy it."

With a warm coffee in her hand, Emmy agreed, and they strolled across the street. The Italian restaurant where they'd had dinner was one of about a dozen places to eat downtown, mixed in among antique shops, used bookstores, places to buy paintings, and a couple of coffee shops. Toward the center was a square with a water fountain, shut down for the winter, and a handful of benches. In the summertime bands played there and flowers dotted the edges.

Downtown Roswell had the feel of a college campus, which reminded Wes about his next collegiate stop, Tributary University. He's always wanted to go after a graduate degree and teach history. He'd put the idea aside after getting his bachelor's degree, put it aside earlier than that by not majoring in history or teaching, but he'd thought more about it after leaving the *North Georgia News*. As a freelance writer and editor with steady work (and making more money than a staff reporter), he could work at his own pace and still have enough time and money to pay for the graduate classes in history that would begin next week. There was so much to look forward to these days!

Wes could feel his heart racing as they approached the square. He desperately wanted Emmy to be part of his future. He stopped and pulled Emmy to his side. His hands felt clammy and he knew he must be blushing.

"What's wrong?" Emmy asked.

"Nothing." He couldn't decide whether to take her hand or bring out the box first, so he attempted both.

"You're cracking me up, Watkins."

He smiled, grasped the box in his pocket, and pulled it out.

But Emmy's attention was diverted. "I don't believe it. Look!" She pointed to the opposite side of the water fountain.

A girl was sitting on a park bench, talking to a guy. The guy was standing, but Wes knew what would come next. He watched the guy lower himself to one knee. The girl put her hands to her face, then extended her hand and let her boyfriend, now fiancé, put the ring on. Then they embraced.

"I don't believe it either," Wes said, deflated. Even with the frigid wind blowing in his face, Wes felt the blood drain from his cheeks. And when he turned, his heart sank.

Emmy was staring at the box in his hand. "Wes, no, I—"

The ring felt heavy.

Then everything happened at once. Emmy's phone rang. Wes thought he saw tears as she turned away to take the call. The hospital where she worked needed her for a shift in three hours. She'd have just enough time to drive from Roswell to Talking Creek, an hour and a half away, change, and get to the hospital.

Wes didn't say a word, didn't move. The ring was still in his hand. But everything else felt like it was slipping away. Before she left, Emmy said something about meeting back in Talking Creek to talk, not to make any rash decisions. She gave him a hug, a strong one, but there was no warmth in it for Wes. He pocketed the ring, sat on the ice-cold walkway of the square, and marveled at how quickly a storybook ending could change.

Chapter 2

Emmy didn't hesitate. Once she received the paramedics' inbound radio report of a suspected stabbing victim, she phoned upstairs to alert the OR and prepped two other nurses while readying a room.

"Sue, you've got airway breathing." Emmy was the shortest person in the ER by at least half a foot, but with her experience as a US Army, then National Guard medic, she was used to belting out orders and being obeyed promptly. "Henry, you handle circulation. I'll take the head-to-toe exam."

The ER doors whisked open ten minutes into the New Year and a rush of cold, winter wind whipped through the hallway. Two paramedics wheeled in a wounded man, groaning.

"What's the report?" Emmy asked without looking at Wayne, one of the paramedics. They'd worked together enough to establish a routine with the more serious patients, for whom seconds were more precious than formalities. She searched for the wound as she listened. "Henry, get an IV in him." Often it was hard to find where the victim had been stabbed or shot. Blood was everywhere, and it was vital to find the wound and put pressure on it, clamp it if need be, before sending the patient for surgery.

Sue had done her airway check and given the thumbs-up, then stepped away. She was still uneasy in high-stress situations, and Emmy was trying to work her along slowly and build up her confidence.

"You need me?" Dr. Jessup poked his head into the room where the three nurses were working.

"Not yet," Emmy said. "Just found the wound. Won't need a clamp."
She applied pressure.

Traumatic situations were old hat for Emmy. Her first taste had come in
an ER in Rome, Georgia, where she finished up her nursing degree. A lot
of the surrounding area was full of old mill towns and blue-collar types, a
population used to rough playing, frequent bar fights, and constant DUI-
related accidents, which made her job a busy one. Emmy quickly learned
to balance compassion with determined grit and earned a reputation as a
no-nonsense floor commander. She didn't take no for an answer, and she
didn't look for gratitude among her patients or coworkers, developments
that would serve her well halfway across the world.

After her stint in Rome, she was deployed to Iraq as a medic with the
army. The treatments were less fluid but more traumatic. She traded in
her proficiency with heart attacks, petty fights, and elderly falls for gun-
shot and shrapnel wounds and horribly burned limbs. Calls to family were
a world away, and the patients received Purple Hearts with their check-
out papers. Medics in the field, nurses at aid stations, and doctors at the
hospitals drastically cut the mortality rate of soldiers in the field. She'd
made so many tough choices under the threat of mortar shells and snip-
ers that now, at the ER in Talking Creek, Georgia, or on maneuvers with
the National Guard unit she joined after her active duty tour was up, she
felt a relative calm.

She was usually one of the first to get the call to work an extra shift,
and she normally didn't mind—the clinical work was still exciting to her.
Plus she was single. Or at least not married. But today she'd come in not
to put in extra hours but to try to run away from a decision she wasn't
ready to make.

What started as a wonderful New Year's Eve dinner in Roswell with
Wes a few hours ago had dissolved into, what, exactly? He'd brought the
ring out but hadn't asked, hadn't gone down on one knee. *Because you said
no right away,* Emmy chided herself. Her stomach tightened at the state
she'd left him in, but she needed time to collect her thoughts before she
tried to repair the wounds she'd inflicted on Wes.

It had all happened too fast. It wasn't that her feelings for Wes were jumbled. She loved him. And she didn't just dole out the word *love* either. She'd experienced it once before, in high school, but that relationship made all future ones more difficult. Through college and most of her twenties, Emmy kept love idle and locked away. Unimpressed with the men around her, she chose to shrug off any commitment in favor of endless rounds of flirting. Most of the men were either shallow thinkers or too driven in their careers to worry about relationships anyway. A handful had simply looked good in a pressed shirt and gelled hair, she admitted. She suspected, though, that her choices had been by design. She hadn't wanted someone who truly deserved commitment, so she spent much of the last few years on one-and-done dates.

Wes had been different. He hadn't wooed Emmy with a flair for adventure or a flashy smile or an all-out blitz of love letters and flattery that she knew waned with all couples over time. He tried, of course, but the words never flowed quite right for him. He was much better with a pen. His comedic timing was slightly off, and he was extremely self-conscious about his appearance and the lifestyle his diabetes required. But he was open and honest and, most of all, caring. He hadn't rushed their relationship, hadn't asked for more, emotionally or physically. Emmy thought the puppy-dog look he gave her would eventually go away, but now, after seven months of dating, it hadn't. The puppy-dog love and affection was still there and now was something of a solid foundation. This, Emmy realized, was what she'd wanted out of dating. To brush off the superficial and scrub away the fluff to get to the important stuff, where Wes shined.

Which made what she'd have to tell him so heartbreaking.

"We're ready to go." Her colleague's pronouncement startled her out of her momentary trance.

With IVs in, monitors hooked up, and the wound identified, Emmy moved the patient into the elevator and up to surgery, where the OR docs had already scrubbed in and were waiting. Only three minutes had elapsed since the man was brought in. As the OR doors shut behind her, she took a minute to collect herself. With someone's life on the line, it was easy to immerse herself in an emergency and ignore the wounds in her real life.

She walked back through the OR doors toward the elevator, shuddering as the impact of rejecting Wes's proposal settled inside. She was torturing the only man she had truly cared for in her adult life, and it wasn't his fault. Part of her wanted to call Wes immediately, but she didn't have time to explain. The talk would have to come after her shift. By then, maybe she'd have a plan for telling him why she'd said no, to make him understand, to figure out if she could tell him everything.

Emmy realized she had wrapped her arms around her chest to collect herself. No more time to reflect. She reworked a loose strand of hair back into her ponytail and entered the elevator, heading back to the ER.

Chapter 3

Paul Gavin stared out the window of his small office in Tributary U's liberal arts college, into an empty quad. It was the same view he'd enjoyed for the last twenty years as a professor in Tributary's history department. The first week of January always held excitement and promise. Gavin enjoyed watching the walkways and lawns fill with traffic, its oaks fill with leaves and the flower beds alive with color as winter turned to spring. The barren quad was but a starting point each winter semester, and he looked forward to beginning his instruction and watching wisdom grow with the season.

At least, he used to.

Paul Gavin sighed and turned to the letter on his desk. Handwritten, well worded, as precise as a regimental maneuver in the field. Two decades of teaching at Tributary's liberal arts college, down to this. The last sentence stared back at him:

It has been my honor and pleasure to serve as a faculty member of this university, but upon deep reflection and an honest appraisal of my health, I hereby enter retirement.

Paul's eyes watered. His health wasn't what it used to be, sure. His legs ached all day, his hands required loosening at regular intervals, and his morning runs had become walks. It was a sad fact that it would only take a few more years to make those walks morning shuffles. But he'd never concerned himself with the deterioration that comes with age. He'd focused only on eating the right foods, hikes and long walks, and keeping his mind active. For a seventy-year-old, he was long in the tooth, but it was a sharp tooth.

The truth was he just didn't have the heart for teaching anymore. Losing his son, Michael, to cancer had taken a lot out of him. He wasn't ready to admit it then, but now, after more than a year of reflection, he knew Michael's death had altered his course, left him somewhere off a well-worn path.

He rose, paper in hand, to do . . . what, exactly? He wasn't a hesitant man. He'd been an army officer, and a good one. He'd made tough decisions under fire, held the hands of comrades as they died, but what he gripped now pained him in a different way, and he couldn't quite pinpoint the reason.

He'd done some good work, hadn't he? For more than forty years, he'd instructed young men and women in some capacity. First as an army officer, molding fresh recruits into competent soldiers who could stay together even as the bullets flew and the world around them exploded. Then as a teacher, shaping the minds of the youth in the Tributary University classrooms, preparing them for their careers and families.

He looked at the pictures on the wall—his wife and children, degrees and awards, and the soldiers he'd known and some he'd watched die. His office was spartan save for those few decorations and a window overlooking the quad.

"What shall I do, Lord?" he said, his head bowed and eyes closed. He still gripped the paper. No answer, but he'd known many seasons when God's plan was silent to him. Like David, his heart ached for an answer to his troubled heart. He sighed, felt very tired, and sat back down.

Someone knocked on the door.

"Come in," Paul said, and Wes Watkins obliged.

"You're late."

Wes looked at his watch. "I'm five minutes early. And school doesn't start back until Thursday."

"No, you are one minute early, by my time, and my time is the only time that counts for graduate assistants. And one minute early is nine minutes late. I want you here ten minutes before a set appointment, understand?"

Wes nodded, his eyes on the floor, a little less fight in him than what Paul had become accustomed to.

Wes had become something of a family friend. They'd met when Wes was reporting for the *North Georgia News,* assigned to one of the most delicate stories in Talking Creek history—to write the obituary, and give the eulogy for Paul's son, Michael, whom Wes had never met. It was Michael's last, impossible request, but Paul did his best to honor it, opening Michael's life to Wes, who at the time suffered from a severe case of cynicism.

Michael was a town hero—he'd been a football star and a decorated war hero—so no one wanted to hear anything but the best of him. Unfortunately for Wes, that wasn't the story Michael had in mind. So after almost a week of investigating, Wes discovered both the good and bad of Michael, and with it his own better and worse traits. Michael intended, it turned out, to make people look at themselves a little more closely, and the town of Talking Creek and Wes himself eventually worked out their own feelings about the town hero and each other. Paul knew that Wes had done some soul searching as well and had determined to change course and become a graduate student in Tributary's Department of History.

It occurred to Paul that Wes might be crushed if he learned that Paul was retiring before the semester began, asking the department if an assistant professor could handle his courses. Then Paul realized that if he didn't help guide Wes, he'd be disappointed too. Wes was something of a mentoring project, and Paul knew he was at a crossroads. Even though Wes had come a long way, Paul recognized he still had some work to do with his relationships and with himself.

Isn't that what God put you on this earth to do? Paul asked himself. *To be a compass for young men like this?*

"I'm disappointed you're only working on your degree part-time," Paul said, sliding his resignation letter in a drawer. "You're getting one class credit for assisting me with grading papers, and you're only taking one class this semester, my American Civil War course, correct? Nothing more?"

"Have to pay the bills," Wes said. "I'm editing for monthly magazines and writing for a quarterly. This first semester I'm testing the waters to see what I can handle."

"And writing a great deal for my class, if you still choose to take it." Paul opened another drawer in his desk. "Well then, I will give you a head start on your first course as a graduate student." He tossed a folded map on the desk, which Wes opened and studied.

"The Atlanta Campaign, for your *lone* class," Paul said. "I will be focusing on it almost exclusively, as this isn't an introductory course to the war. I love this campaign and being able to focus on specifics is why I love my upper-level courses. For you it means a couple more research papers and a thicker reading list, I'm afraid. For the entire class, though, I will offer a field tour of the campaign. We'll start at Rocky Face Ridge this Saturday. I'll e-mail directions, time, and location this afternoon. From there we'll visit Snake Creek Gap, Cassville, the battles surrounding the Marietta area . . . we'll cover it all, and hopefully those who join in the fun will have some moments of inspiration for their term papers. How does that sound?"

"Intense," Wes said. He smiled.

"Something funny?"

"Ironic, I guess," Wes said. "I was actually thinking about e-mailing my father about Civil War battlefields. He has some letters that his father, my grandfather, kept that were passed down from an ancestor who fought in the Atlanta Campaign."

"Is that so?" Paul said, trying to act surprised. In fact, Wes's dad, Ron, and Michael had become good friends. Paul had met and spoken to Ron several times. He knew about Ron's letters and a few other things. He also knew Wes had started talking to him again.

"One of the few topics we can get through without awkward silence," Wes said.

"Why not invite him?"

"To what? Our class?"

"The tours."

"You're serious?" Wes's voice dropped as his eyebrows arched.

"Why not? I have guests on these trips all the time. Old soldiers from my army days and colleagues and whatnot. They're open to anybody— Tributary has even had the tour times published in the *North Georgia News* travel section. I've rehearsed what I'll say enough times to give you the whole thing right here and now. Your father wouldn't be a distraction is what I'm trying to say. With those letters, perhaps the two of you could prove invaluable to the other students."

"I . . . I don't know. . . . He might not be able to make it. He works odd hours."

Paul knew he was trying to think of a reason against it. "Never hurts to ask."

Wes set the map down and looked at Paul. "You're doing it again. Setting something up. Just like Michael did."

Paul put up a hand. "No, I am not. Do you see a folder with contact names and a written letter? I never set anything up to begin with. That was Michael. And you had the option of saying no, remember? You were the one who brought up your father and the letters, which is why I extended the invitation. You cannot get more constructive than college class work. I won't even offer you extra credit for it, so there."

Wes furled an eyebrow. Paul realized he was a little too defensive in his response. He reached over and took the map back. Still, his spirits were rising, and he felt the same anticipation as he had years before, instructing at the army's Ranger School. Young recruits and grizzled vets were sent out into the field loaded with gear, hampered by too little sleep, with a mission to accomplish, all for the honor of being pinned with a Ranger tab. *Academia's aim is for its pupils to come out more disciplined and knowledgeable than when they entered,* he thought. Wes was after an A. But Paul hoped Wes would get more than a nice grade for his school records.

"I will e-mail you and the rest of the class directions," Paul said. "It was just a suggestion, young man. I do not appreciate those looks from civilians, much less my students, and even less so my graduate assistants. I'll be giving you more than a fair share of marching orders this semester. This one is all on your own."

Chapter 4

Checkmate?" Emmy set a mugful of freshly brewed coffee on the table in front of Wes, who was using his history syllabus as a cover for not looking Emmy in the eye. Wes took the coffee but wondered if he was supposed to ask what checkmate she was referring to. Their relationship?

"The Pilgrims, silly," Emmy said, pointing to the Pilgrim salt-and-pepper shakers Wes had been shuffling on her breakfast table. She bent down to pet her beagle, Baxter. "It looks like you've got a great game of chess going with my out-of-season salt and peppers."

"Oh. Never learned chess. Wasn't smart enough for it. I'm more of a checkers guy."

Emmy's giggle sounded forced. She set her own coffee on the table and sat down. But not before touching Wes's hand. Was that a sign? This felt like their first few dates, hanging on every word she said, trying to read her mind by her voice inflections, what she laughed at, how many times she smiled. He'd gotten used to not looking for those signs as much. Not that he was good at reading them. Emmy would have made a great poker player.

Pictures of their developing relationship were still on the walls. His face still took up space around Emmy's family, fellow nurses and soldiers from her tour in Iraq. There hadn't been a box of pictures and books waiting at the front door. And she hadn't posted anything on Facebook about their trip to Roswell and his failed proposal, hadn't changed her relationship status.

"Tell me about Paul," Emmy said. "How did your meeting go? Does he already have you writing *War and Peace* for his class?"

"Yeah," Wes said with an edge in his voice. This was not the discussion he wanted to be having. But he knew Emmy would get to their relationship when and only when she was ready. "He's set up a tour of Atlanta Civil War battlefields and wants me to bring my father along. Ron's kept some old Civil War letters from our family."

"That could be a good opportunity for you and him to reconnect."

"We've done that," Wes said.

"But this would be more than coffee or a five-minute phone conversation. You could get to know him better."

What's to know, Wes wanted to say. Ron was pretty much in the same spot where he started when Wes was born—working as an appliance repairman. Ron and Janet had gotten married in college. Ron worked two jobs—a warehouse job and then as an appliance repairman—to pay the bills. He dropped out of college while Wes's mom got her degree, and instead of picking it back up, he transferred his credits into a life of petty theft and drugs, eventually graduating to working at a chop shop. In the few conversations they'd had, Ron said he was different now. But it didn't change the divorce and embarrassment and anger built up from all those years. Besides keeping the Watkins last name, out of defiance more than anything else, Wes hadn't wanted anything from Ron, and still harbored doubts about reconnecting.

"I didn't come here to talk about my father, Emmy," Wes said, finally looking into her eyes.

Baxter sensed the mood in the air and grunted, then trotted to the couch and curled into a ball to let the people work out their differences on their own. Wes looked down at his hands to see that they were holding the salt-and-pepper Pilgrims hostage. He let go and let his hands retreat under the table, his cheeks turning pink with embarrassment. He'd been confused and quiet the moment he'd received Emmy's phone call after his meeting with Paul to come over to her apartment to talk. She hadn't said about what, only that it was important. Was this what she really wanted to talk about? What in the world did she want? Her voice on the phone had been even, not without warmth but also not highly emotional.

If Wes had to pick one trait that bothered him about Emmy, and there were few, it was her ability to shut off her emotions. The poker player again. Of course it was a superb talent to have for the ER and her line of work. Having been in a war zone, she'd probably honed it to professional proportions. But sometimes it unnerved Wes that she could turn off her feelings like a faucet, like their relationship could dry up at any moment.

Like right now. He wondered if that's what she was doing. "I'm sorry. It's—I've got to ask—I don't want to small-talk everything to death before we mention the elephant in the room. Are we breaking up?"

Emmy looked at him, considering the words. The longer she was silent, the deeper Wes's heart sank into his chest.

"I don't want to break up, Wes."

"But you don't want to get married."

Emmy was silent.

"I proposed too soon, didn't I?" Wes continued. "It's just—we haven't gotten into a lot of fights, and you win most of them anyway. We've already said we love each other. We aren't in college. We've dated seven months. There's no one else I've been this close to, and I'll be the first to admit I'm not a relationship guru, but I thought we were doing all right."

Wes had to force his mouth shut. He wanted to tell her it felt like he had an open wound that was only getting worse. That he wasn't eating or sleeping well. That he thought he'd patched his life together quite well since going freelance, since meeting her at the Gavins' barbecue, since using her encouragement to enroll at Tributary. That he felt like it was all about to fall apart—the lynchpin was coming loose, and he didn't know why.

"You've been great to me," Emmy said.

"And I love you." Wes studied her eyes.

"I love you too." She met his gaze and reached for his hands. "I really do, Wes."

"But . . ."

Emmy sighed. "There is no but. I need to tell you something. It's not that I want a breakup. That's the last thing I want. But maybe I've been a bit spooked. We watched that couple get engaged in Roswell, and it spooked me."

"Why would that spook you?" Wes's eyes were wet, and he was mad about that, about showing emotion. He pulled his hands away and rotated his coffee mug, eyes down, blinking hard.

Emmy didn't notice because she was out of her seat now, gathering her thoughts. "The timing's not right."

Wes stood and gripped the back of his chair until his knuckles turned white. "Okay, so back to square one?" His voice cracked. He looked at Emmy for a tear, a sob, something, but all he saw was her jaw tighten.

"No, it's not that at all," she said. "I'm leaving. Part of the reason I got spooked is I didn't know how to tell you. My unit got activated. I'm going to be deployed in May."

Chapter 5

To enter his mother's three-bedroom ranch in Alpharetta, you had to get past the bear. Carved from an oak tree and about chest high to the average person, Smokes (as his mother called him) was an impulse purchase on a visit to Gatlinburg, Tennessee, a tourist destination in the Smoky Mountains. Smokes wasn't alone. Inside resided a mule's saddle converted into a wall mirror, purchased in Ellijay; a bookshelf made from half a canoe, bought in Big Canoe; a year's supply of vanilla-scented soap from a Sautee outpost store; and in the pantry mason jars to use as glasses, bought years before somewhere Wes's mother, Janet Stover, had forgotten.

Wes patted the front-door guardian. "Smokes, you got anything to share before I knock? Everyone else seems to have picked the New Year to lay their surprises on me."

He'd had a week of tough news. But his mom had news of her own, informing Wes she was packing up and moving to Nashville in a month, so Wes put a freelance writing assignment on suburban Atlanta school districts on hold and used his last day before graduate school to visit. On the car ride over he tried to pull himself together before she had a chance to grill him. He took a deep breath and knocked.

When Janet, smelling of vanilla, opened the door, she immediately wrapped her arms around him. She was almost forty-eight, her hair long enough to wear down or put in a ponytail if she was working. She'd lost a little weight and a little color. Her kidney issues forced her to watch her health as much as his diabetes made him watch his. Her high cheekbones were what gave her away as a knockout, and Wes remembered his pride at having such a beautiful mother at school open houses and rec league baseball games. It helped compensate for having one part of the parenting equation absent.

It always puzzled Wes that Janet never remarried. He could count on one hand the number of dates she'd had, or bothered to tell him about. He'd encouraged her to date, wanting some kind of decent example of a man to blot out the smudge that was his father, but his mom didn't have the heart for it. She put all her energy into church activities, signing up at least once a year for mission work overseas. In that part of her life, she was an inspiration. But sometimes Wes felt she was just going through the motions in the rest of it, like someone punching a time clock each day, and for the longest time he'd wished she'd jolt the pattern. And now she'd gone and done it.

Janet released Wes and put her hands on his shoulders, meeting his gaze.

"No," Wes said, shaking his head. He'd informed Janet of his plans to propose to Emmy, and after much prodding, even divulged how he was planning to do it. Wes calling his mom the next day to tell her Emmy said no felt like coming home from basketball tryouts without having made the final cut. "I'm not here to talk about her."

Janet ignored him. "Emmy doesn't deserve you if she's going to treat you this way."

"I'm here—"

"You reap what you sow, you know."

"You called me about something else, so let's—"

"And really, what kind of person lays a big 'I'm deploying' on someone as an excuse to dump him?"

"We didn't break up! And anyway—"

"You didn't? Wes, you can't let anyone string you along, and that's all she's doing until she finds another boy to play games with. Maybe she already—"

"You're moving, Mom," Wes said, his voice sharper than he would have liked. "Okay? Let's focus on why *you* called."

She bit her lip. "Probably not the best time to tell you, as it turns out, but thank you for coming."

"Of course," Wes said. The news that his mother was moving to Nashville would otherwise have shocked him, but with the week he'd already had, it was actually pleasant to be able to digest a turn of events.

The move made sense for a number of reasons. She rented her house so all she had to do was give notice. She already had a job with health insurance and everything lined up at a distribution company her brother owned. Most of her family lived in the Nashville area, aunts and uncles who were mostly strangers to Wes. He was glad she was finally getting along with her family. Her parents and her siblings had remained cool toward her since she'd gotten pregnant with him out of wedlock. And for all her wonderful characteristics, Janet was an extremely stubborn woman and had been the one to shut off communication until her mother's health worsened a few years before. The family had called a truce to care for and then mourn their mother.

The olive branch, it appeared, was now permanent. *Good*, Wes thought.

They moved into the living room and sat on the couch.

"It's just God's perfect timing," Janet said. "The day my company here sent out the memo to everyone saying they'd be downsizing, I felt paralyzed. But then I prayed that God would use this as an opportunity to lead me in a new direction, and he did. It just so happened your aunt Glenda called, and we talked about everything. She mentioned your uncle having an opening, and right after I hung up I got down on my knees and prayed, thanking the Lord."

Janet wasn't bashful about her faith. Every decision, every event in her day, whether layoffs or a parking spot, she traced back to God. Her faith was kind of a headfirst dive Wes never felt comfortable with—even now, despite his growing faith.

"How are you feeling?" Wes asked, hoping she'd divulge the reason for her weight loss.

She smiled. "Like I'm on top of the world. Can't you tell?"

"What would you have done had the job not opened up in Nashville?"

Janet looked a bit deflated. "Does it matter? God would have gotten me to Nashville—just like he wanted you in Talking Creek."

"No argument on that. He and I are still figuring out how to . . . talk with each other, but I got that message loud and clear. Well, is he going to help with the move?" Wes smiled as he placed the joke.

His mother playfully jabbed him in the ribs. "Money's not too tight, but it'd be nice if you could help me move the boxes in the Roswell storage bay at some point in the next few months."

"Absolutely," Wes said, holding his palm out for the keys. "You wouldn't happen to have anything left from Ron in there, like Civil War letters his dad had given him?"

The lines on Janet's face crinkled. Wes felt like he'd just taken a swipe at her, although that hadn't been his intent.

"No," she said, her voice flat and controlled. "Why?"

"I need to run something by you. For one of my classes, there will be field trips to different battlefields around Talking Creek and then south toward Atlanta. I'm planning on going to most of them, but my professor nudged me in the direction of inviting a certain guest along for the trips. Somebody who's got a batch of letters from a Civil War soldier who fought in the Atlanta Campaign."

"Ron. No, I don't think we've got any of his stuff." She grew silent, and her eyes dropped to the floor.

Wes didn't like the expression on her face. "I don't have to invite him. I was actually hoping he'd left the letters in some random box we had. Maybe I'll just meet him in Marietta and get the letters."

Janet sucked in a deep breath. "You should invite him."

"Really, it was just a stupid idea because Ron's been bugging me over e-mails and I was trying to impress my professor. I'm not even sure I want to spend all that much time with Ron. This stuff is still new to me, even after we reconnected last year."

"It's okay to reconnect," Janet said. "You don't have to base it off of how I feel about him."

"So you won't be mad if we do this?"

"No," she said, but Wes heard the strain in her voice. "You should do it. It's ironic that the history bug hit you, because it skipped him. He was more into cars. I remember how big of a history buff his father was. Ron didn't get into it as much, but one summer he took you and me and his beat-up truck, when you were little, up to Lake Allatoona, to hike the trail and then over to a nearby marina. He rented a pontoon boat, and I got a good tan on the sundeck. I remember that. Would you be going there, to Allatoona?"

"Possibly a last stop," Wes said. "That battle, well, when it was a fort and not a lake, happened after the Atlanta Campaign, kind of leading into Sherman's March to the Sea and Hood's retreat into Tennessee—"

Janet put a hand up. "I'm remembering the suntan and when I could fit into a skimpier swimsuit, not the history lesson."

Wes chuckled. "Fair enough. So it's okay if I do this? Just say the word and I'll nix it. Happily."

"It's fine. Go ahead and learn something about your own past while you're at it."

Chapter 6

Professor Paul Gavin opened the door to his classroom and marched to the whiteboard like it was the middle of the semester and not the first day of class. He wore a blue sport coat with a dress shirt underneath, both neatly pressed. His walk was purposeful, military. Paul knew exactly what he was doing. It was a practiced technique—one drill sergeants used on new recruits to command their immediate attention. He scribbled his name, the class description, and the time before he turned around to survey his pupils, hands on his hips.

Ah, the sweet perfume of fear, he thought. His Civil War course was offered for undergraduates and graduates alike, but most of the seats were taken up by twenty-year-olds.

As an army officer, Paul's reward had been to watch raw recruits grow from wild-eyed, undisciplined messes to strong, capable decision makers. Devastating when they didn't make it home from the war or were crippled by it. He still remembered their names—a dozen in all under his command in Vietnam who'd fallen. There would have been more if he hadn't learned from the mistakes that led to their deaths, but still he mourned that there were any mistakes at all. That burden of remorse was shared by anyone who owned a command. His son, Michael, had known the guilt of leading in war too.

The successes, though, were like fuel for the soul. Paul had kept in contact with the soldiers under his command who'd grown into business owners, police officers, and even the mayor of a small Louisiana town.

Their stories warmed and encouraged, and he soon found his calling was instruction and not business or politics, which he'd considered initially. The army's final gift to him was a free education to help him realize his second career. So for more than two decades, he'd been playing the part of a potter—forming, sculpting, and creating vibrant minds.

Or so he convinced himself. The yawns and halfhearted essays and speeches rankled him as much as a soldier bumbling over a compass and map on the training grounds. In his first few years as a professor, he constantly reminded himself that undergraduates weren't soldiers, that scolding would only take them so far, encouragement farther. And so he had honed a new tactic: building students up without breaking them down.

It was a necessary change because the civilian sector was different. Some students just couldn't be broken—at least in a way acceptable in academia. They were fiery, sure of themselves, and always quick with an opinion of the world, whether right or wrong. Paul often wondered what a few weeks of basic training would do to them. Yet eventually disagreeing with his younger, commissioned-officer self, Paul saw that these students didn't always need the military blueprint to find success in their studies and careers.

He reminded himself of what he called the Great Campaign: a teacher with twelve students in a back corner of the world's largest empire ushering in the greatest kingdom of all. Fishermen, tax collectors, and zealots—now *there* was a group to mold! This man's students were poor learners. They stumbled over themselves, denied their teacher, watched him die, and lamented their losses until they regrouped in a cause that would spread across the earth, to every corner.

God could create what he wanted out of each person's path. There were many routes and many examples throughout history. That was what attracted Paul to the subject of history in the first place—seeing the way God moved through everything.

"The Civil War. Our Civil War," he began. "I'll be brief, this being our first day. I will say my piece, and then you can be on your way to read the syllabus and take a nap—which, judging by our student lounge and the quad during springtime, is all most of you do anyway."

The remark elicited a few snickers.

"The first order of business is this sign-up sheet for our Civil War tours," he said. "Understand, this is not extra credit. You will not get brownie points, but you will get a thorough education on the Atlanta Campaign— which can only help you in your studies. History surrounds you; I suggest you take advantage of it."

He set the paper down at the first desk of the far left row but made eye contact with Wes as he did it. He stifled a grin as he thought about the high hopes he had for Wes . . . and a few surprises he had waiting as well.

"Can anybody tell me who the great leaders of this time period were?" He held up a finger. "Stop. Erase. New sheet. This is a subjective exercise; there is no wrong answer. Tell me, whom do you think were the great leaders?"

"Lincoln," said a boy with bushy hair stuffed under a backward hat.

"Good." He wrote *Lincoln* on the board.

"Lee," said a girl in the front row.

"Grant." "Stuart." "Sherman." "Longstreet."

Paul kept writing. "A lot of generals mentioned this morning. How about some others?"

"Seward," someone blurted out.

"Lincoln's secretary of state," Paul said. He recorded all the names that came in; when the cache dried up, he turned to the class. "Now I want everyone to participate. Who hasn't given a name?"

Wes and three others raised their hands.

Paul frowned when he saw Wes's hand. He'd learn quick about Paul's expectations for graduate students, and that their friendship outside the classroom wouldn't have any influence on his grade. "Okay, let's have it."

Names from the late answerers included a future president and even George Pickett, who led an entire division to its doom on the third day of the Battle of Gettysburg. Paul's marker sliced the air to end the snickers.

"This is subjective," he reminded the class. "And it allows me to bring up a good point in a minute."

Paul pointed the marker like a garage door opener at Wes.

"Joshua Chamberlain?" Wes said.

"A professor turned soldier," Paul said. "I went about it the opposite way. Indeed, Mr. Watkins, Chamberlain is perhaps the most important of the names on the board, at least for one critical hour in the war."

"More important than Lincoln?" someone asked.

Paul nodded. "This is a subjective exercise, but allow me to elaborate. On the second day of Gettysburg, Joshua Chamberlain and the Twentieth Maine held the far left of the Union line. Had they been turned, the entire Union army could have been wrapped up. The war very likely could have tipped toward the Confederates. A nation's history tied to the fate of one regiment and ultimately one man. It wasn't of his choosing, but he rose to the occasion."

Paul set down the marker and leaned on his desk. "Chamberlain's story is a case study in history. Great men and women become great not just because of their talents but because of opportunity. Ulysses S. Grant was a drunkard and a business failure, but when the war started, his perseverance overshadowed those faults and led him eventually to the White House. Had Robert E. Lee hailed from any state other than Virginia, would he have chosen to fight alongside the rebels? He was in the United States Army, after all. Even Lincoln, our greatest president in my opinion—his nomination came about after a tumultuous Republican vote. Had it happened in modern times, Seward very well might have been president."

Paul surveyed his class. He'd hooked their attention, and he allowed himself a measure of pride. Perhaps there was more in the tank than he'd thought only a few days ago. "Chance. Luck. Whatever you call it, if there is one theme I want you to grasp in this class, it's that often our own histories come down to these moments. Some are of our choosing. Some aren't. And sometimes the odds are impossibly stacked against us. It's not the what I'm interested in with this topic as much as the how and why. Remember that for your papers and presentations this semester. Focus, people. You'll need to focus."

Chapter 7

Emmy ignored the fatigue in her legs and the searing pain in her lungs. She shut out the fact that it was exactly one week since she'd rejected Wes's proposal. She wasn't even thinking about her deployment, not until she finished her run. In the cold, heavy air, she strained, sprinting for the final turn of the Talking Creek High School track. "Focus," she managed through gritted teeth, forcing her eyes on the turn and not the stopwatch. "Focus."

Her left foot planted at her imaginary finish line and she clicked her watch to stop. She refused to bend over; instead, she put her arms on her hips and sucked in a full measure of fresh, rigid air. Then she looked at the time.

Two miles in seventeen minutes—well within what she'd need for a good score on her fitness test, but well *outside* what she'd set for herself. In high school and college she could hover around two miles in sixteen minutes without much difficulty, and she'd lost only a little bit of that edge in preparing for her first deployment. This was a slide back.

A minute later Lynn Gavin rounded the track, every bit as spent as her niece. "You don't look happy," Lynn said when she'd caught her breath.

"I need to get my times down."

"Why, are you trying out for the Special Forces track team?"

Emmy rolled her eyes. "I just need to be in shape is all. Long hours and sleep deprivation and everything. I don't want my fitness to cause any problems with acclimation."

"You're deploying, not running a triathlon! I could have kept Addy in the car instead of dropping her off at her grandparents' and raced you around this track in our car and still lost."

Emmy shrugged and began to stretch. "Want to go another mile?"

Lynn groaned. "You've cornered the market on self-punishment. No thanks. Was the to-do list giving you the evil eye or something?"

Emmy grinned. "Ever since I received the orders for deployment. Won't let me make a cup of coffee before giving me a cup of guilt."

Lynn nodded. "And running gets your mind off things. I remember all about that," she said. "The closer you get to the big day, the more signatures you seem to need and the more chores need to be done. But all I wanted to do was spend as much time as I could with Michael before he left. Which reminds me . . ."

Emmy followed Lynn to her sedan in the parking lot. Lynn pulled a well-worn duffle bag out of the trunk.

"It was Michael's," she said. "Just in case you need one. We won't be using it."

"Wow, Aunt Lynn, I don't know what to say." Emmy had one of her own, but she understood what her aunt was doing. It was part of her grieving process, giving portions of Michael's life to others to help them. Lynn had ventured away from the foster-care retreat she and Michael had started, and moved into a townhome on the outskirts of Talking Creek. After a short-lived career as an elementary school teacher, she realized her true passion and delved into a new degree and a new career as a physical therapist. But there were still holes, would always be holes, where her husband had been.

"Our unit will go to Fort Gordon in March for some training, and that will be a good test run. I'll use this to pack," Emmy said.

"Do you need us to take care of Baxter?"

Emmy shrugged. "Probably not. I already had a caretaker in mind—for Baxter and for all my bills and stuff, and if he doesn't want it, then I'll probably ask my parents."

"Wes?"

Emmy nodded and Lynn laughed. "He has no idea what he's in for," Lynn said. "That dog will clean out his kitchen before he knows what's hit him."

"Wes joked a time or two how it's odd I've got my apartment baby proofed. I've warned him, but he's pretty sure of himself because he has the fenced-in back yard at the house he rents. But that only eliminates one pitfall—the digging and the barking take even more mastery. Only one way to find out if he's beagle worthy."

"Babysitting a dog is a big step," Lynn said. "So are you two pretty serious?"

"Well . . ." Emmy decided to tell Lynn about the botched proposal.

Lynn sat through the story with a hand cupped over her mouth. At the end she let out, "Oh my."

"Oh my is right," Emmy agreed. "I can't even begin to tell you how touch and go it's been. Maybe him taking care of Baxter will show him that I don't want to walk away from the relationship. I'm just not ready to think about marriage. This is the most serious relationship I've been in. But I had just found out about the deployment the week before."

"Would you have said yes if the circumstances were different?"

Emmy sighed. "I don't know. I mean, it was a little sooner than I expected. I've wanted to say yes when he asks, but I thought I'd have everything in my life accounted for beforehand, you know? There's still this pile of baggage, and the deployment only adds to it. He thinks it's because I'm deploying. And maybe that's part of the reason. But I haven't told him about the other reason, and I don't know what he'd say."

"You deserve a good life, Emmy. Don't keep beating yourself up for something that happened a long time ago."

"There's always a chance . . ."

Lynn turned toward Emmy. "That you'll knock on their door like you do every year, but this time you'll get a different response?"

Emmy looked away.

"If that's what you need, you have to deal with that first," Lynn said. "But you shouldn't postpone your life because you're not perfect. No one is. Marriage isn't something to rush into, and it takes hard work, tears and sweat and all that—but we're not perfect when we say our vows, and we're certainly not perfect a year or a decade or fifty years later. You can't wait to live until you've patched yourself up when we're all springing leaks every day. And you should know that better than most: you've made a career out of sewing people back up! You make a living giving people second chances. You're part of the answer to their prayers. Don't you think God hears yours too?"

Chapter 8

Wes wished his father would calm down. Ron couldn't keep his hands still. He cracked his knuckles and wiggled his fingers, and his eyes darted from the interstate to where their cars were parked on the shoulder and back to the interstate again.

The arrival of a highway patrolman didn't help. A cold sweat broke out on Ron's forehead, and Wes wondered whether his father would pass out or run. There was plenty of room for Wes's Camry and Ron's Ford F-250 to park away from the passing highway traffic, but sitting on the edge of an interstate was generally frowned upon.

The patrolman eased his car onto the edge of the highway shoulder, where the gravel met the grass.

"Please don't flash the blues," Ron mumbled. "If he flashes the blues, we're in trouble."

"Blues?"

"Lights," Ron said, stuffing his hands in his pockets and looking at the ground like it would somehow mask his identity. "Always a bad sign when they flash the blues."

Wes shook his head and took a few steps forward. The officer opened his door and waved for him to stand still as he got out.

"Car problems?" the officer said.

"No, sir," Wes replied. "Civil War class. My professor is giving us a lecture on the Civil War. Well, when he shows up."

An oversized rig rushed by, and a gust of air nearly knocked the men over.

The officer chuckled. "That'd be Professor Paul Gavin, of Tributary U, correct?"

"Yes, sir. How'd you know?"

"Not his first Rocky Face Ridge lecture, boys," the officer said. He tapped his car's roof. "He'll be along shortly?"

"Now, as a matter of fact," Wes said.

Paul had arrived with an SUV full of students. He hopped out and shook hands with the officer.

"Kids still interested in this stuff, Paul?" the officer shouted above the highway noise.

"It's got guns and violence, don't it?" Paul said, and they both laughed. "So we've got, what, about ten minutes on the roadside to fix our cars?"

The patrolman grinned. "Sounds about right," he said. He turned to the crowd of college students. "We keep our roads safe around here and are happy to help distressed motorists. Would sure appreciate it if when ya'll consider your charities for the year to keep our Highway Patrol Fund in mind."

Paul waved a handful of highway patrol stickers and sign-up cards in his hand. "An excellent idea, I'll mention it again before we depart."

Wes counted heads. Seven including himself and Ron, who had floated farther away from the patrol car when Paul arrived and was surveying the highway median, with his back to the officer, like it was the most interesting thing he'd ever seen.

The patrolman didn't seem to notice. He smiled at Paul and nodded for him to join his students, then revved his engine and peeled away from the shoulder.

And thus Professor Paul Gavin began his classroom oratory as eighteen-wheelers and SUVs zoomed by on I-75 south to Atlanta. His students huddled closer on the grassy shoulder while Paul seemed oblivious to the danger only feet away.

"As you see," Paul said, pointing to the jagged mountain that stood watch over them and the highway, "Rocky Face Ridge is a formidable obstacle, and Confederate general Joe Johnson had it well defended from

Union general William Tecumseh Sherman's advance, though he didn't need as many troops to do so."

Ron leaned over to his son. "I can't believe he's giving a lecture on the shoulder of a highway."

Wes shrugged. He still wasn't sure how to act around Ron. The two hadn't been on speaking terms from middle school until a little over a year ago, mostly because Wes wanted it that way. He'd ignored his dad's letters and e-mails, and would have continued the stonewalling, not for the turn of events where he learned about Michael Gavin and his connection with Ron.

Another eighteen-wheeler zoomed by, sending a rush of hot wind onto the huddled group that brought Wes's attention back to Paul's lecture.

"Sherman, of course, had no intention of attacking Rocky Face Ridge with all of his forces. Whereas Johnson had the terrain, Sherman had the numbers and could split his forces."

"Isn't there a trail where we can do this without the big rigs?" Ron yelled over the noise and in Wes's direction. "Maybe we should have agreed to coffee instead of this. Or you could have introduced me to that girlfriend of yours."

That stung. "Can't we just listen to the lecture?" he said through clenched teeth.

"I'm trying, but the sound of cannon—cars—is getting to me. Was either side using cars during the war?"

Wes heaved a sigh and continued to ignore him.

"I just wanted to make one more point," Paul said, raising his voice, "and then we can proceed to the nearby markers on the walking trails and off the highway. Johnson had pinpointed every path he thought Sherman would cross and deployed accordingly. But despite his best efforts, Sherman surprised him by sending one of his most trusted officers with a force through Snake Creek Gap and out the other end of Resaca. By all accounts the Atlanta Campaign started here, but it was only a feint by Sherman. Turns out Johnson didn't know as much of his opponent as he thought he did."

★ ★ ★

Following Paul's highway lecture and a quick stop at the battlefield markers, the professor and class departed, and Wes agreed, somewhat reluctantly, to have lunch with Ron at a nearby sports bar in the center of Dalton's outlet malls. While families roamed the open shopping center with oversized plastic bags stuffed with discount shoes, jeans, and jackets, Wes watched his father scarf down a massive bacon-and-cheddar hamburger. He felt like he was watching a college freshman who'd discovered the all-you-can eat buffet at the dining hall.

And the comparison didn't stop there. Ron was built like he worked summer jobs with a moving company or in construction, arms toned, shoulders large.

Ron wiped his mouth with his forearm, leaving a small smear of ketchup. "This. Is. Awesome. Why didn't you order a burger?"

Wes pulled out his Accu-Chek. "I'm a salad man now. Emmy's helped with that." He regretted mentioning her immediately.

"Women'll do that to ya," Ron agreed.

Wes glanced at the bag beside Ron's chair. He wished the meal could be over and the letters in his possession. He looked long and hard at Ron. "Let's not talk about women, since you left Mom for another one."

"Wes, I surely didn't."

Wes's eyes hardened.

"Honest truth," Ron said. He leaned forward. "I mean it. I met a girl once the papers was signed. But I wasn't the one wanting them signed, and that girl was a few months afterward."

"Look, if you want me to take your word over Mom's, forget it. She wins, seeing as she raised me."

Ron swallowed hard. "This is going to be a tough trail to hike, I can see."

"Did you expect anything else?"

"I guess I didn't," Ron said. "Here it is though. I'll say this piece and won't bring it up again. Set your boundaries and tell me whatever it is you need to tell me if it helps; I'll take it. Bet I deserve it too. I just hope and pray through all of this you'll find it in your heart to forgive me someday."

Wes stood silently; then Ron reached down to the bag. He pulled out a series of folders.

The Civil War letters. Wes sat back down. "Let me guess, one at a time as we tour each spot?"

Ron gently placed the folders on the table. "The real ones are dated, but my dad made copies, handwrote them. They're both in there. Take them and keep them if you want."

Slowly, Wes reached for the letters. "We can try this again on another day, but I'm about full."

He paid his portion of the bill at the counter, put the letters on the passenger seat, and drove away.

Chapter 9

Back at his place, Wes dug through the top shelf of his closet for the bundle of letters his father had written him from in prison and out—some from his high school and college days, but most having come in the last few years. Very few of the letters Wes had actually read. He placed them beside the Civil War letters on the edge of his breakfast table. His plan had been to start reading through the Civil War letters and get a proposal over to Paul, but what Ron had told him in Dalton at lunch bothered him.

Something about Ron's giving him the letters without any strings made Wes think his father was telling the truth about the other woman. But why would Janet lie? And how dare Ron ask Wes to forgive him after walking out when Wes needed him . . . when his mom needed him. It was a huge request, one he knew he'd have to come to terms with eventually.

And that was the problem. He'd reconnected with Ron on account of his interactions with the Gavin family. Digging into Michael Gavin's life and finding the good and bad had shaken Wes, forced him to be less cynical and more empathetic. But Wes admitted that while grace and forgiveness were concepts he searched for and wanted to accept, they were easier to see and accept at arm's length in the lives of strangers than in his own life with someone who'd failed him.

"Well, there it is," he said, half to himself and half in prayer. "You don't want me observing anymore. You want me participating. Paul wants me to read these war letters. You want me to read both. I get it."

But he reached for neither. Emmy called it a walk in faith when events not of his making forced him to examine things he wanted to ignore. She would know, being so involved in the healing process, seeing how the body mends itself through the pain of surgery and rehab. The body did most of the work, but the person had to do some less-than-appealing things to help it along, she'd said. And while Emmy must have found those painful processes clinically fascinating, Wes wanted nothing to do with them.

The letters sat there, expectantly. "Fine," Wes said. "I could have been nicer at lunch. Let's see what you had to say to me in high school." Wes reached for the bundle of his father's letters. The top letter was one Ron had written when Wes was a junior in high school. He remembered it, one of the few he'd bothered to read. The letter was short and apologetic, but there wasn't any substance to it. In the two paragraphs written, Ron made excuses for himself and his situation. Wes tossed it to the side. Methodically, he went through the next half dozen or so—encompassing his senior year of high school and freshman year of college, and found them to have the same basic structure—a halfhearted apology, explanation of where Ron had gone wrong or an excuse for his latest trouble. It wasn't until he got to the letters postmarked in 2006—when he was a sophomore at Georgia—that the letters grew thicker. He squeezed the edges of the envelopes underneath and found them to contain a similar weight. He threw the older, lighter letters in the trash, but took out the first lengthy one from 2006, and began to read.

> I wanted to start this letter out "In the beginning," but I realized how much it sounded like the beginning of the Bible, when God started this whole thing rollin'. I guess it'd be kind of fitting though, if you think about it. I'm writing this as kind of a fresh start, just like Genesis is a fresh start.
>   Are you surprised I can write? Runs in the family. My daddy, your granddaddy, was a business executive and wrote for a few historical journals, so that's where the genes

come from I think. A buddy of mine thought it'd be helpful to get all of these words down on paper, like saying it in ink is better than letting it swim in my head—a shallow pool, granted, but that's the idea. I've got a lot of time on my hands, and while I don't feel like I owe much to anyone, you're the exception. I owe you a fresh start. An "in the beginning." But we don't get to do that, so the best I can do is give you an open book on how I got to prison and how, despite having me as a dad, you got to where you are. I'm hoping and praying this turns into a conversation one day and this letter doesn't end up dusty and unread in a closet, but what I pray and what I deserve don't always mesh.

In the beginning, your mom had a routine. She'd nurse you at 2:00 AM, and if you didn't fall asleep, she'd poke me in the ribs. So most of my memories of you as a newborn were me waking up and seeing you crying in the outstretched arms of your mom.

Your mom would dump you into my arms like a cafeteria worker scooping mashed potatoes onto a student's plate, and then she'd collapse into bed. You didn't seem to notice. We'd pace the tiny living room of that apartment, going back and forth over the cheap carpet until I got you properly soothed. I was usually beyond exhausted at this point. A full-time job at a shipping warehouse in the early morning nearly wiped me out. Coming home to the pressing needs of a newborn and bills and a very tired wife trying to finish a degree . . . it was all I could do to survive the day.

But I'd look down at you, your tiny mouth sucking away on a pacifier, that little red spot on the top of your forehead that the doctor said would go away within a year (a swan's kiss, I think they'd called it) . . . you were so delicate, so impossibly vulnerable. After my baby shift and as I left for work, I'd check and recheck the front door to be sure it was locked. I wanted a platoon of marines to guard the walkway. This wasn't an "I'll protect my buddies in a bar fight" kind of an instinct, but an "If anyone so much as thinks about harming my child in any way, they're in for trouble" response.

It was amazing, really, how much your mom and I changed because of you. A year before you showed up, we were two college students partying at local bars and dancing into the morning hours, occasionally fitting in classes and studying. Our cares consisted of keeping enough money for a cab and high-enough GPAs to stay enrolled. Now Janet was occasionally fitting classes in between nursing a baby, and I had dropped out of college to work. But my full-time job at the warehouse didn't seem like enough. We were late on bills and close to maxing out our credit cards. We'd downsized to a cramped, two-bedroom apartment on the sketchy side of town, and I was driving my daddy's old pickup truck. But we still didn't have enough money left over to pay for something nice, like a babysitter and a movie.

I'd ask myself why it was so hard and decide I needed coffee. But work was still three hours away. "No, I need a beer," I'd say. I should have seen the warning signs. I'd look at the fridge, thinking long and hard about the chilled six-pack beckoning. My father had always had a drink after work. I remember hearing his Buick come up the driveway, my heart melting as the engine cut off and his slick dress shoes hit the carport. I'd run to the door to give him a big hug, get one in return, then continue watching cartoons while Dad nursed a vodka and tonic in the kitchen, talking to my mom about office politics at the plant and how close he was from senior VP to moving into the C-suite of the company.

But I wouldn't go for the beer—at least not then. I'd think of my dad and what he'd think of me, and at first it kept me away.

When I first told my dad Janet was pregnant, he wouldn't look me in the eye. We were sitting at the breakfast table, looking out on his well-manicured lawn and leased Buick. Mom crossed her arms and mumbled something about what her friends at the club would think—like somehow her tennis partners and lunchtime gossipers had a say in matters—but then she recovered and offered motherly support. She even offered to stay with us once you were born to help Janet. Dad walked out—to his study with the mahogany desk and thick doors that had shut out me and the rest of the world for as long as I could remember. I can still feel the vibration of those doors slamming shut. He later said that I'd never turn out to be anything but a loser, that I'd ruined all he'd built for me. At first I did everything I could to prove him wrong.

I'm not telling you all this to make excuses. I just wanted you to know that we had a start, you and I, and it wasn't a bad one. Those early mornings I'd look at you fast asleep in my arms, with the knowledge that my wife was sound asleep, the power and water were still on, and the realization that I needed a second job.

Chapter 10

Donald Stewart's handshake was the kind practiced over dozens of years, thousands of business meetings. A handshake that didn't back down. Emmy had seen it wipe the confidence out of a car salesman when she and her father went to buy her first car. She'd seen it deployed over church pews and at church potlucks. It was backed up by steely gray eyes you couldn't look away from but sure wanted to.

"You mean to tell me," Donald Stewart said to Wes, "that you asked for my daughter's hand in marriage but didn't bother to call me first?"

Emmy saw the edges of Wes's eyes strain to look to her for support, but he held up, continuing to meet her father's gaze. She'd briefed him as they held hands and walked three blocks from the church parking lot to downtown Talking Creek where they were to meet her parents for Sunday brunch. They wore coats and gloves but the temperature wasn't as chilly as the last couple of weekends. Emmy was certain the proposal would probably be her dad's first topic, even though it was ten days old. Her father was a traditionalist. Emmy's wish to suspend the decision was irrelevant.

"I know, sir," Wes began. "I should have. It was a spur-of-the-moment thing."

"A man doesn't buy a ring spur of the moment."

"Well . . ." Wes stammered.

Her father opened the door as if to say he'd made his point, and in walked Emmy and her mom followed by Wes and Mr. Stewart. They were seated quickly, having beaten the rest of the church crowd, and ordered sweet teas and waters. Wes dug out his Accu-Chek from his pocket and stuck his finger. He checked his numbers, as did Emmy, who leaned in and gave him the thumbs-up when she saw his blood sugar was in a good spot. They noticed surprised looks from Emmy's parents.

"You guys knew he was diabetic, right?" Emmy said. Her parents nodded and set their napkins in their lap and fidgeted with their silverware to the side. After ordering their food and exchanging updates about work, Emmy drew a deep breath, which hushed everyone. Wes reached for her hand underneath the table, could practically feel her pulse racing through her veins.

"Thanks for driving all the way from Athens after the early service. There's a lot going on right now that I wanted to update you on," she began.

"Besides Wes proposing?" Mr. Stewart said. Wes curled the lower part of his lip in and bit down.

"Yes, and I didn't ask you to come here to talk about that," Emmy said in a sharp tone that quieted her father. Even Emmy was surprised at her retort. She needed a moment to collect herself before continuing. Wes squeezed her hand again.

"I'm going to be deployed again. This time to Afghanistan."

Wes watched Emmy's parents as she went into the details about her deployment. Mrs. Stewart took a deep gulp of water, set it down, and placed her hands neatly in her lap, although her throat worked itself up and down during Emmy's briefing. Mr. Stewart's face hardened to concrete, like he was listening to a business transaction gone wrong and waiting for his time to negotiate.

"You've already served a tour," her father said as soon as Emmy finished. "You shouldn't have to go again."

"That was with the Army, dad," Emmy said. Wes felt her lean slightly toward him. "This is with the Guard."

"And afterward, you'll be done serving?" Mr. Stewart said.

Emmy let go of Wes's hand and rubbed her temples with her palms.

"We just wish you would have gone into something less dangerous, Emmy, that's all," her mom said.

"I don't know, from the stories she tells me, Rome's blue collars were no walk in the park, and there are some mean-looking bumpkins who can get into a lot of trouble around Talking Creek," Wes said, trying to deflate the tension. "She can handle emergencies. Truth be told, I kinda use her as my body guard."

Donald grunted, either at the joke or entertaining if the thought was true, Wes wasn't quite sure.

"Well, we'll support you, of course," her mom said, then quickly turned the conversion toward family updates of Lynn and others in Talking Creek. They worked through the idle updates as lunch came and went. When it was over, Emmy hopped into the back of her father's Cadillac to visit some more at her apartment, but not before giving Wes a tighter-than-normal hug and promising to call him once they left. Wes drove back to his place and spent the early afternoon researching for his history class and dictating an interview he did for a freelance article on puppy vaccination guidelines for veterinary clinics. By 3 p.m. his eyes hurt from the computer screen. His phone buzzed on the table, startling him. The caller ID said Emmy in bright green letters. He smiled.

"Hey you, kinda early to be calling," he said.

"That was painful," she said.

"I thought you handled it great at lunch. I know it's not easy dropping a bombshell on your parents."

"I'm glad you were there," she said. There was a pause. "Do you mind coming over?"

"Uh oh," Wes said. "Did you save a surprise for me?"

"Sort of," she said. "But it's a good one. I think. Well, you'll have to come over."

"Not until you give me a guess."

Wes heard a laugh on the other end, which he took as positive and encouraging considering the day Emmy had just had. "It's a thirty-six-pound commitment I wanted you to watch over for a few weeks while I'm gone."

"Say what?"

Chapter 11

The thirty-six-pound commitment howled as its sensitive nose caught wind of a squirrel or rabbit off the Talking Creek hiking trail. Wes tightened his grip on the leash, but Baxter's torso was all muscle, and it was all Wes could do to hold the stout beagle in place. Emmy watched nervously as Wes tried to get Baxter under control.

"So, you probably don't want to watch him now," she said as Baxter transitioned from a deep-throated howl to a high-pitched bray.

"I didn't say that." Wes tugged at the leash again and brought Baxter to his side, then placed his palm on the beagle's backside and forced him into a sitting position. Baxter looked up, tail wagging and whimpering, but Wes didn't budge.

"This is usually the part where I try to bribe him out of hunting," Emmy said, fishing a treat from her pocket. She held out her hand and Baxter engulfed the treat in one fluid motion.

"Man, that dog can eat," Wes said. "He's gonna eat me out of my pantry."

"If you don't want to, I understand. I was going to ask my parents, but . . ."

"I'd love to watch him," Wes said.

Emmy smiled wide and hugged Wes. Baxter sensed opportunity and tugged at the leash again, but Wes kept his hold. Emmy brushed back a strand of hair and laughed at herself. "You wouldn't believe me, but telling my parents the news actually went better than the last time."

"When you deployed to Iraq?"

"Yep," Emmy said, letting the p pucker out for emphasis. "My dad was livid, ready to march to whatever recruiter had brainwashed his little girl and tear up the enlistment papers. Most of my life they had dreamed of me going to the University of Georgia or Emory and eventually to med school or law. But by my senior year in high school, it was obvious that wasn't the route I was going to take, so I enrolled in a community college in Rome. My grades there were good enough to transfer to UGA, so I think they got their hopes up again, but there was no nursing program at UGA, which is what I wanted after my two-year degree was completed, so I finished my nursing degree at the community college. Then I signed up as a medic, which was hard for them. My dad couldn't fathom the idea of me in a war zone. Of course, what parent can?"

"The ones too busy messing up their own lives to support yours," Wes said. "In his own way your dad was showing you love."

"I know," Emmy said. "I know he loves me. Mom too. I think they just poured it into the wrong things sometimes. Soccer camps and soccer equipment and traveling teams, by high school I was exhausted from it. But all the other kids had their own career tracks and soccer and AP classes were mine, even though I told them over and over that's not what I wanted. 'You're smart enough to be a doctor,' they told me. Well sure, but what if that's not what I want?"

"Do you think you chose nursing, and being a medic, to rebel?"

Emmy laughed. "No, I definitely did my rebelling in other ways, like clothes. For a while I'd dress in the hideous outfits almost like I was a porcupine wanting to stick anyone who got near me. Nursing was a way for me to . . . heal. I think of my job as the front line of the healing process."

She stared at the trail ahead, then snapped out of the daze. "Enough about the glory days. We should get going. Don't you have a term paper to write and papers to grade?"

Wes groaned. "Yes, but I'd rather stay on this trail with a pretty woman and a howling beagle than misspelled historical names and a red pen. This graduate work is totally eating into my freelance time too. I almost missed a deadline with the veterinary trade magazine I edit. Then I go from puppy vaccination guidelines to the Boston Tea Party. I've got a stack of papers to grade from Paul's—Professor Gavin's—intro American history class. He goes over them too. I thought the point of having a grad assistant was for professors to dump part of their workload, but I get the feeling he's evaluating me more than the class."

"What makes you say that?"

"After I turned in the first batch of graded quizzes, marked in red, he put them in my box at the college mail room, marked in purple, to show me what he wanted—which he could have gone over beforehand or during our weekly meetings. Plus, he's already pushing me in my Civil War class, and it just started. I'm the only grad student in the class, so I'll have the most homework and writing, but he already rejected my first proposal for the semester paper. Replied within five minutes of me e-mailing it last night. I didn't think he had a computer at home. Something's up."

Wes explained Paul's interest in Ron's Civil War letters and in Ron and Wes attending the Civil War tours together. "I bet he'll reject more paper proposals too," he said. "I think he's trying the same tactics Michael used with me, trying to get me talking to Ron more. But of course I can't prove it."

"That's one way of looking at it—cynically," Emmy said.

"Can't help it. It's the reporter in me. They kind of drill into you to ask questions, to be skeptical of quick answers and shallow stories. It's served me well a few times—even served me well with Michael when people were reluctant to open up about his faults. We've all got faults, just a matter of drilling down to them."

"And then what?" Emmy said, with a hint of defensiveness.

Wes looked in her eyes to try and read her intent.

"I just think you need to give people the benefit of the doubt," she said. "Michael had his reasons for keeping secrets, didn't he? And doesn't it always seem like the people who get hurt the most in anything are the ones you love?"

"Is this about us?"

Emmy looked like she wanted to backpedal. "I guess it could be," she said. "I told you no when you proposed, but you're still here. I hurt you, Wes, and you gave me the benefit of the doubt, and I'm grateful. I'm glad we didn't break up. But there's more than just me. Your dad hurt you. Everyone in our lives eventually hurts us at some point. Do we give them all a second chance?"

"Isn't me being here proof of that?"

"Yes. I'm trying to ask, what does it take from each person before we let down our guard?"

"Time, circumstances, I don't know."

Emmy gave a weak smile. Wes felt another awkward pause coming. Then Emmy grabbed his hand, giving him her best mischievous grin.

"Circumstances change, Wes Watkins," she said. "Sometimes you've got to learn new tricks. I've got you for another few months before I deploy, and I don't want to be talking about weighty things all the time. How about we circle back to the car and I can tell you all about Baxter's daily schedule and see if you're still committed to babysit him while I'm away."

As if on cue, Baxter tugged at the leash on the hunt for another animal, nearly sending Wes headfirst onto the trail.

Chapter 12

Wes, let me tell you something, this gal is one of a kind. You find a gal like this, you don't ever let her out of your sight."

Wes waited for the punch line. Instead, Ron patted the hood of the car in front of them on the Calhoun used-car lot off of I-75. "A 1970 Plymouth Barracuda convertible—with Hemi. This thing could drop-kick a Mustang, Camaro, or Corvette any day of the week. Talk about fast. This baby could race!"

"Could it beat out a cavalry charge?" Wes asked sarcastically. "Because you know, that's why we drove up here."

"Yeah, buddy," Ron said, ignoring the sarcasm. "We'll get to the Resaca battlefield. Paul will wait for us."

With no mention of the last visit's meltdown, Ron had wholeheartedly agreed to do another Civil War tour and answer some questions about the Civil War letters. He met Wes in Cartersville on the fourth Saturday in January so the two could ride up together, had a friend named Otis Lattimore drop him off. Otis didn't say much and didn't make eye contact. After he left, Ron surprised Wes with one request: a stop at this used-car lot, after which Wes could ask as many questions about the letters and his grandfather as he wanted.

Ron circled the Barracuda. "These racing stripes mean business."

"Yeah, and the neon green color, real classy."

Ron gave Wes a sharp look.

A screen door slammed as the lot owner walked out of the trailer, jingling a set of keys in his hand.

"You boys interested in the Barracuda?"

Ron looked at Wes like a kid in the toy aisle of Wal-Mart. "You want to take it for a test-drive?"

"Was hoping we'd get in some time on the Civil War letters."

"We've got time."

"I can't."

"It's easy, my man," the owner said. "Simple signature and you two can cruise for a few."

"I don't know how to drive a stick," Wes said.

Ron looked shocked. "My own son—" He stopped himself as Wes's eyes narrowed. "My own fault too. Should have been me giving you driving lessons. Makes perfect sense why you drive a Camry."

"What's wrong with a Camry?"

The lot owner and Ron looked at each other as if to share a hidden truth.

"Well, ya'll can look around," the owner said, realizing no sale was going to happen with these two. "You have any questions, give me a holler."

Three cars, two trucks, and ten minutes later, Wes and Ron hopped back into Wes's Camry and headed toward Resaca, a few exits down. Ron seemed less uptight; the used-car lot had been like a drag on a cigarette.

"Kind of ironic," Ron said, gazing out the window at the rolling North Georgia hills. "Your grandpa was a big history buff. Me, not so much. I loved to get my hands on something, fix it, make it better. Wanted to understand its inner workings. When I was young, though, this was how we'd spend some weekends, riding to a Civil War battlefield in his red pickup because he didn't want to get dirt, bugs, and miles on his Buick. Anyways, when I got older, close to driving age, he'd take me to that type of dealership, the only kind in those days, and listen to me squabble about Mustangs and Barracudas. Even bought me a used Corvette, a little worn, but I spent a good few months fixing it up and driving it around like a king—till he sold it and dumped his pickup on me, that is. Now it's reversed itself."

"Wish I remembered him," Wes said.

"Pa should have visited more—your grandma did before she passed on a few years after Pa had his heart attack. He and I were at odds for a bunch of different reasons that don't mean all that much now, like that Corvette, and me being a daddy sooner than he'd like. I don't think it squared with the image he wanted out there as an exec at a manufacturing plant. Wanted the kid who went to college and got a degree and had a white collar that wasn't stained with mechanical oil or grease, you know?"

"So you like to visit car dealerships as a way to remember him?"

"That," Ron said, "and I'm looking for something."

"Even with your brand-new F-250? That's a thirty-thousand-dollar vehicle."

"More than that," Ron said. He turned to look at Wes. "Son, I find this vehicle, I trade that F-250 in a heartbeat. Done deal."

★   ★   ★

On the outskirts of Resaca, a narrow, two-lane dirt road led to a gravel parking area. Nearby stood a faded metal historic marker that said "Snake Creek Gap." A few other cars pulled up and then Paul began his lecture.

"What we saw at Rocky Face Ridge was just a diversion by Sherman. No one in their right mind would attack a fortified mountain in force—at least not at that stage of the war. We'll get into Kennesaw Mountain later. For now, though, Sherman had the luxury of having the equivalent of two armies—three, in actuality. So he used the Army of the Cumberland to entertain Confederate forces at Rocky Face Ridge, while his main focus was this gap here."

Paul pointed down the country road that led through the mountain range. "Snake Creek Gap," he said with emphasis. "What could have been. Sherman sent his favorite subordinate, General James McPherson, and the Army of the Tennessee through the gap and into the rear of the Confederate lines in Resaca. The flanking maneuver couldn't have gone better. In fact, it was too good. McPherson could have destroyed the railroad and thus the Confederates' supply route and created a trap as they retreated south. But he hesitated and waited for reinforcements, while the Confederates withdrew from Dalton down here to fortified positions, leading to the Battle of Resaca. The fate of thousands tied into that hesitation."

"Lots of coulda, shoulda, wouldas already, and the campaign is just getting started," Wes said.

"You're correct," Paul said. "Sherman's undoing here was that the man he relied upon, his most trusted general, failed. Unfortunately, because of the human element, the best plans don't always work out."

Chapter 13

Some folks don't have a moment that changed everything for them . . . they have just a slow crawl to wherever it is they got to. Unfortunately for me—and I guess you and your mom—I went big with the changes. Basically I can point at one day. It's a day I've wished I could take back many times, but that ain't how it's set up, and I did promise I'd tell you how I got to where I was.

So my plan had been for one more. I'd moved up in the world, from the warehouse to driving a truck for a bottling company. I put in a full shift moving soft drinks across the county until the early afternoon, and in a couple hours I'd be on the clock again, working appliance repair until the wee hours. I wanted a break, so instead of driving home to your mother and you, I went to the nearest sports bar. Warning bells should have gone off that I was finding more comfort in stale peanuts, pool tables, and shots of whiskey than with my wife and one-year-old baby, but all I could think about was taking the edge off. So I ordered one more.

"It's 3:00 PM," the bartender told me, between wiping glasses and putting them in cabinets.

"Right," I replied. I downed the last of my shot of whiskey, let it burn in the back of my throat, and let out a satisfactory sigh. I didn't take the cue, went ahead and told him my sob story, about how I couldn't relax at home, that my wife had recently taken a frowned-upon stance any time I'd come home with a six-pack of Coors. There wasn't enough room in the fridge for my frosty beverages, what with all the kid supplies she stuck in there, like we're a full-service day care. I didn't want to mistake a cold one for a juice box, so there I was at 3:00 PM at the local sports bar.

I confided that I dreaded going home, where Janet would complain about this bill or those hours and I'd swallow the lecture and look at the clock and leave a few minutes early toward more toil.

At this point I realized the bartender had moved into the storage room. So I started chatting up a guy who'd just walked through the doors. Kept his head down, body language was telling me he wanted a Bud, but not that kind of bud. At this point, maybe a voice in the back of my mind was telling me to slow down—no, stop altogether, order a soda or a water and sober up before getting behind the wheel, or I wouldn't be much good at the appliance shop, and I enjoyed that work. It reminded me of when I was a kid, taking apart and putting back together old radios. I had a talent for it. I could lose myself underneath a car's engine or the bright light of a workshop bench, like you did with your crayons and blank sheets of paper or Golden Books.

But then another part of my mind chimed in, the loudmouth. It told me enough of the ham sandwiches instead of steak dinners, enough of diapers and savings instead of the sports car classifieds I'd always had my eye on. I still had your grandfather's old Ford, and I wanted out, wanted to inhale that new-car smell and not his old aftershave and shoe polish. It told me I hated clipping coupons instead of being out with the boys, all of them fresh from college with degrees and a bona fide career ladder, while I was wallowing in minimum wage and fatherhood.

I swallowed my responsibilities and signaled the bartender, who had returned "'Nother one, sir!"

"I call you a cab if you have one more drink," he said to me.

"It's 3:00 PM, by your watch. I don't need a cab," I replied.

"You don't need another drink either. Your call: drink and a cab, or water and the check."

So I gripped the shot glass and gave him a piece of my mind. Went something like this: "Man, I'm getting a little tired of people giving me options like that. 'Either do this or do that, your choice.' You know what? I'm a grown man. I decide what I do. I decide what I eat and what I drink and where and when I do it! Not you or Janet or some stupid boss who wants me on weekend shifts. No one is going to tell me what I have to do. And you're a bartender, for crying out loud. Serve me my drink, or leave me alone."

Then I slammed the shot glass down on the bar. Unwise. The bartender put the phone back. "Go."

I should have left. "'Scuse me?" is what I asked.

"Get out of here before I call the cops."

"I just want another drink. You're the bartender. Do your job."

"Get out—"

Before I could process my stupidity, I grabbed my shot glass and tossed it at the mirrored wall. The glass shattered, spraying tiny particles all over the back of the bar. Larger sheets of glass from the mirror crashed onto the floor. My mouth fell open. So did the bartender's. He looked at me, the glass, and back to me. Then he reached for the phone.

See how quick it happens? I pleaded for him not to call the police.

But the bartender kept dialing. Good for him, in hindsight. I would have done the same thing had I been sober and sane. I panicked and ran outside to the parking lot. I heard the shout from the bartender. A million thoughts rushed through my head, none of them good. Jail, court, losing a job, hearing it from Janet. When you were older, you'd hear about this, for sure.

I considered running. I looked at my daddy's old, beaten-down truck and thought about scooting home. But I took one whiff of myself and one shaky step in that direction and gave up. Plopped down on the sidewalk. I was tired of life and I'd barely even started. I wondered how you get clean of an arrest record.

Sirens blared in the distance, the entrance to the bar burst open, and someone stomped toward me, probably the bartender, probably with a bat for protection. My dread, though, came from an upcoming phone call. Things had been stressful enough. What would this do? Would your mom hang up on me, let me wait it out down at the county jail? I drew a deep breath, tried to hold back the tears of desperation and fear, and actually did something right before it all began to fall apart. I turned to face what I had done.

Chapter 14

Wes made a midweek trip to his mother's new place on the outskirts of Nashville in just a shade over four hours. The car ride was scenic—descending Missionary Ridge into Chattanooga and then back up the Cumberland Plateau toward Nashville. It was early February, and in a month there'd be signs of life sprouting from trees and the ice from the plateau's rocks turning to cascades beside the roadway. He used the time to think about the term paper looming over his head, and Emmy. But five minutes into talking with Janet, he wished he'd pressed Janet more in January about how thin she was and why she was moving to Nashville. Maybe he wouldn't have been caught so off guard . . . again.

"It's time I faced this disease, Wes."

He had known about the illness most of his life. Knew its acronym as a child: PKD. Studied its full name in high school: polycystic kidney disease. He knew it was hereditary. You were either born with it or you were in the clear. He didn't have it; the diabetes had been a surprise.

But Wes's maternal grandmother had PKD. She'd lived a long and fruitful life until her sixties, when the disease began its slow, painful siege. First it robbed her of her mobility, then her lifestyle, and eventually it took her life like her mother before her—and probably countless others in her family tree. It wouldn't die with her though; she'd passed it on to two of her children, one of them his mother.

He held Janet's hand as she told him the PKD was starting to get the better of her—her blood pressure was rising, she felt nauseated more often, she found herself breaking out in hives, constantly itchy. And she had become anemic.

Wes connected the dots in his head. "Is this why you moved?" he asked, suddenly suspicious.

She nodded. "Dr. Benewitz has treated my sister for the last few years. Your uncle Cory's business—we checked it out before I moved, and he was able to get me on their coverage without too much of a fight. We were really lucky. Well, there was a fight, but he wouldn't tell me how bad it was or if they raised the rates. He's pretty determined to beat PKD with what it did to your grandma. So I've got a support system up here. Not to say that I didn't in Georgia, but this is family. It's good to be home."

"What's your treatment involve?"

"Well, long-term I'll need a new kidney," she admitted. "The doctors in Nashville have put in a request for a transplant. But not right away. It's just time to plan. The doctors will check my creatine levels, and if they get to a certain point, I'll have to go on dialysis first."

"You're getting a transplant," Wes said, his grip firm and his face grim. "Sooner rather than later."

"It's not like the drama shows, Wes. I have time." She stroked his hand. "What's the Bible verse I always told you when you'd get frustrated with your diabetes? 'Don't worry about tomorrow, today's troubles are enough'?"

"It's in Matthew. But Mom, you *are* getting a transplant."

His throat constricted. How was it that his father, who had abandoned him, owned a criminal record but a clean bill of health, while Janet—the parent who'd tucked him in at night, made him PB&J sandwiches, and held the throw-up bucket when he got the flu—was facing serious health complications now?

Janet pulled out a tissue and blew her nose. "Wes, honey, lots of people are on dialysis. Your grandmother was for years."

But Wes knew complications from a dialysis treatment had led to his grandmother's death when he was seven. He remembered traveling through Middle Tennessee and its farmlands into Nashville and downtown for a brief visit at the hospital. Then they whisked him away to his grandparents' house, and that was the last he'd seen of her.

"I don't want you on dialysis. I will give you one of my kidneys."

"Absolutely not. I don't know if they'd even let you with your diabetes, but you are not giving me one of your kidneys. I gave birth to you, and there is nothing that's coming back into this body, you hear?"

They laughed together before the conversation got serious again.

"It'll be fine, Wes. God will take care of me."

"And I'll help," he said. "Like a stranded person in the ocean, right? Pray for a miracle but keep rowing in the life raft for land."

"Exactly like that."

"It's almost too much, you know? I mean two months ago I was planning on marrying Emmy. I put a down payment on the ring. My job was good. Graduate school was about to happen. You were good. I was talking to Ron. Everything was fine. Now Emmy is leaving for Afghanistan before the semester is over. She rejected my proposal. You need a kidney transplant. The only thing that seems to still be on the tracks is the Civil War tour with Ron. And if I had to pick one of those to fall through, it'd be that. What is going on? Where is God in all of this?"

"Don't say that, Wes."

"Well, it's an honest question. Where is he?"

"He's there. He's here. He's always accessible with a prayer. You should know more than most how he can turn heartbreak into something better and beautiful."

There was her faith again. She was as quick to reach for it as Wes was to grab a line of questions. She'd used it to soothe him when she administered insulin shots or he got a bad grade at school. She hadn't been much of a churchgoer before the divorce—she'd said as much when Wes was old enough to hear the stories. But she'd found warmth in a local congregation and rooted herself there.

Yet for all her prayers, all her tithing and time at church, she hadn't really addressed the subject that haunted them both: Ron. She could see God in a failing kidney but had never reconciled with her ex-husband, her son's father—had never even tried. God didn't seem to have a place in her relationship with Ron.

Wes stood and walked into the kitchen to pour a glass of water. "I'm not a Michael Gavin, Mom. He was a Christian a long time before he got cancer. I'm not you either. And if I'm supposed to make sense of my faith or whatever it is I'm doing, this isn't helping."

"Maybe this is what you and I both need for God to be more real to us."

Wes sighed. "Okay, sermon's noted. You've got the right attitude, and I don't want to sap it. So why don't we both work to our strengths? You keep praying, and I'll pray a little and work a lot. Nashville isn't all that far from me, and I'll make my freelance and school schedule work. I can drive on my off days and help out with your treatment. And when you do get the transplant—which *is* going to happen—I'll be there to help you recover."

"My sweet boy."

"If it comes to it, I won't be sweet," Wes said. "I'll cuss out doctors and hound the insurance company. I'm going to do whatever it takes to get you better. That is a promise."

Chapter 15

Wes rubbed his eyes and tried to pay attention in class. But he had two things working against him—one, the early, early morning ride back from Nashville to barely make the 11 a.m. class in Talking Creek. And second—Paul wasn't giving a lecture today. Rather, a student was playing a clip of a movie during a presentation. Lincoln, as Wes had dubbed him, flicked the light switch and stopped the DVD.

"As you can see," Lincoln said, brushing his mop of red hair with the remote, "Jeff Daniels was out of options. His men were just about out of bullets, and the Rebs were still coming. So he made a choice that led to one of the greatest victories in American history, and subsequently, one of the greatest speeches given by a president."

He paused and looked at the class, then grinned as he answered his own question. "The butterfly effect—at Gettysburg, circa 1863."

"You're forgetting something," Paul Gavin reminded his student. "Jeff Daniels didn't fight at Gettysburg."

"Oh," Lincoln said. He smacked his head with an open hand. "Right. It was Josh Chamberlain."

Paul nodded. "Joshua Lawrence Chamberlain."

"So anyway, Josh and his band of merry men from Maine, they turned the tide. Had they not been where they were, we might be talking about a famous Alabama regiment that changed the outcome of the war. Pickett might never have charged, Lee might never have wept, Lincoln might never have given the Gettysburg address or been assassinated. Pretty awesome, huh?"

Paul cleared his throat.

"One regiment made a difference," Lincoln repeated. "One leader, one man in a war." He scanned the class, looking for validation. But there were no claps or cheers, just as there'd been none for the others who'd gotten their assigned speech out of the way.

"Very good," Paul said. "As with all of these presentations, I will let you know your grade in private. That does it for today."

Lincoln gave Wes a thumbs-up and a head nod as the class shuffled out of the room. Paul shuffled a stack of papers at his desk, clamped the pile under one arm, and signaled Wes to follow him to his office.

"So, Watkins, what did you think?"

"I'm having trouble finding words," Wes said, easing into a chair. "*Horrible* comes to mind. He bummed half his talk off a movie and the other half off our first class discussion. I didn't hear one other resource attributed."

"I liked that movie," Paul said with a twinkle in his eye. "One of my favorites."

Wes groaned. "You're telling me you approved his paper and presentation because he used a movie you like in his speech? What else do you like, *Braveheart*?"

"Is this in regard to the paper topic I rejected from you the first week of class?"

Wes frowned. He knew he'd rushed through his proposal, and had deliberately waited until the undergraduates started with their presentations and papers to see what their subject material was. He thought his revised proposal, sent the day before he visited Janet, was sound enough. His paper would focus on the letters of his grandfather, Benjamin Watkins, and would include the man's upbringing, maybe where he came from and its cultural and religious foundations, followed by his decision to join the Confederate army.

"My paper will focus on the individual decisions of Benjamin Watkins and how they were influenced by the theater around him—the war, army politics, and also the home front. Although his decisions and the fate of his army are documented history, for Benjamin the situation was very much fluid."

His proposal had been rejected in just five minutes.

> Mr. Watkins,
>
> First, what I like about this topic: you've added the personal element to a larger story. Of all the criteria for this assignment, meeting that objective is the most satisfactory to me. A single figure in a larger drama makes for good reading.
>
> However, I would like you to use that as just part of your story, perhaps devote only a page to his past. I would like to know about his actions, his day-to-day living in the face of such catastrophe. And ultimately, how did the Atlanta Campaign, which helped shape the country, shape him?

"Just seems I'm being held to a different standard."

"A higher one," Paul said. "Mr. Watkins, fairness as you see it is irrelevant in this discussion. I'm the professor, and I set the rules. And I made it clear at the beginning of the semester that as a graduate student you would be judged based on higher standards. What I accept from undergraduates is not the same, nor should it be. The semester paper is included in these standards. And you've got a virtual gold mine of historical information in those letters your father gave you."

The mention of his father dinged an alarm in Wes's mind. Paul had been quick to suggest Ron go along on the Civil War tours and had brought him up again with the letters. The insistence to keep Ron's influence in the class work was unsettling.

"Maybe I was rushed," Wes admitted. "I'll work up another proposal. I was in Tennessee yesterday, otherwise I would have responded to your e-mail."

"Visiting your mother?"

Wes nodded. He decided to tell Paul about Janet's condition. Paul listened intently, waiting until Wes had finished to say how sorry he was, that Janet would be in his and Betty's prayers, and that if there was anything he could do, to let him know. Those statements often rang hollow from others, but Wes knew Paul meant them. He even asked for Janet's mailing address so he and Betty could send their well wishes.

"She's in the Lord's hands, but it doesn't hurt to have encouragement," Paul said. Then his eyes squinted, like he was zeroing in on a thought. "Plus now I know where to send your grades. Higher standards, you know."

Chapter 16

The sound of ten pairs of Nikes planting, pivoting, and sprinting on the freshly waxed basketball court reverberated off the bleachers and into the rafters. The remaining sounds swirling around the gym included high school kids flirting and gossiping, parents lecturing younger siblings or critiquing coaches, and coaches barking orders to their teams in this hotly contested regional game in early February playoff positioning.

Wes sat with Emmy at the top of the Away section of the Calhoun High School gym, well clear of the clustered Talking Creek supporters. Wes typed his game story while Emmy chewed on gummy bears.

"Can you believe that call?" she screeched, nearly spilling her soda. "Nobody laid a hand on him! Unbelievable."

Wes scribbled in a notepad he was using to keep stats. "Ref didn't agree. That hurts. Nate Stroud is Talking Creek's best player, and he's got three fouls now. And maybe you want to tone it down? Being with the reporter, and all?"

"I thought this was a freelance assignment," Emmy said. She shoveled a handful of gummy bears into her mouth and waited for a reply, but Wes just grinned.

"It *is* a freelance assignment from the *North Georgia News*, and it paid for your dinner," he said. "Apparently you didn't eat enough."

"I always have something sugary at a movie, silly," Emmy said with a playful punch to his shoulder. "And seeing as you've taken me to a basketball game instead of a movie, I'm eating my gummy bears . . . so there." She shifted in her seat in mock distance from Wes.

Wes turned most of his attention to the game. Not all of it. Despite the patchwork on their relationship since the proposal, the disquieting feeling that if he didn't keep an eye on her, she might vanish hadn't gone away. He knew that the feeling was more him than her—she had been honest with him about her feelings and the deployment. It just felt weird to have hit the pause button.

"So what are we doing after this?" Emmy said, snuggling back over to Wes. He put down his notebook and wrapped his arm around her shoulder. He wanted these moments, wanted to trap them in a mason jar and put them on a shelf so he'd have them while Emmy was away.

"Don't you have a twelve-hour shift tomorrow?"

Emmy nodded. "But I'm cranking up the endurance factor for deployment. Kind of like a runner trains for a marathon and builds up stamina. Except I eat comfort food before—and after—my training. Which means we can go and do something after this—ice cream, coffee, cookies. I'll burn it off in the ER."

"That's an odd training method," Wes said. "But I can accommodate. Lots of food options in Calhoun, like Dairy Queen and Dairy Queen, or Dairy Queen."

She gave Wes a sharp look. "Or a movie or a bookstore or a sports bar in Cartersville to watch some college basketball."

"Fair enough," Wes said. "I've got to do some quick interviews and send in this write-up. But it shouldn't take long."

Emmy folded her arms. "Better not."

Wes typed a paragraph. "See—it's the middle of the third quarter of a Talking Creek blowout because Nate Stroud is on the bench and I am well over halfway done. Which reminds me, this Saturday, Talking Creek's girls team is heading up to Canton to play, and I can cover it if I want."

"Canton," Emmy said. "One of my childhood friends is now the coach up there, Dina Bowman."

Wes had noticed Athens listed as the hometown in Dina's bio and recognized Emmy's high school. "Want to tag along?"

"Can't," Emmy said. "I'm picking up an extra shift. Besides, Dina and
I haven't spoken in a long time. Unfond memories and all that."

"Of what, Dina?"

"Of high school."

A whistle blew, and the ref ran to the scorer's table to announce another
foul. Wes identified the number of the perpetrator and recorded it in his
notebook.

"Really?" he said, returning to their conversation. "I thought you'd be
Miss Popular, even with your little rebellious streak. You were on homecoming court and the soccer team."

"My rough patch ran from the end of my sophomore year and then
almost all my junior year. Quit the team, didn't play again until intramu-
ral in college. It kinda *was* high school."

Wes felt like he should have known all of this, that he should have had
a conversation about it with Emmy. He realized more and more the talks
they hadn't shared while dating. "Care to tell the juicy details?"

Emmy shifted uneasily on the bleacher. She kept her gaze on the game.
"Broke up with my boyfriend, that sort of thing."

"Gabe, right? A jerk, huh?" Wes couldn't say why, but he felt a need to
measure himself against her past.

Emmy swiveled around almost immediately. "No. It wasn't that at all.
Can we talk about something else?"

"Sure," Wes said, but they didn't. Emmy finished her gummy bears,
and Wes acted like he was putting double the effort into his story, wondering all the while what Emmy was stonewalling about.

Chapter 17

Emmy reached into the dark, fumbling to turn on the lamp. She heard Baxter groan on the edge of the bed. Rubbing her eyes, she checked the clock: 2:00 AM.

It never failed. Whenever she reached into her past, sleep deprivation followed.

Dina Bowman. Had Emmy made a few different choices, they could have been lifelong best friends, the two most athletic girls in their high school class. Dina had led the girls basketball team to state finals her junior and senior years, winning it on her last try. Emmy's soccer club had been poised to do what no other school team had accomplished: win regionals and make the play-offs. But it fell apart when the best forward ever to walk through their high school's doors turned and walked back out, into a deep, self-absorbed abyss.

Emmy's teammates never forgave her. Understandable. One or two might have had scholarship offers with the exposure of the play-offs and playing next to Emmy. They'd worked their way up together through the summer rec leagues and JV ranks and on to varsity and were poised for great things, but the season fell apart without her. Emmy remembered walking the halls on game days after she quit the team, with her former teammates wearing glares with their soccer jerseys. Emmy remembered those awful glares and how they only got worse as her state of mind worsened.

She rose from bed and shuffled to the kitchen to make some decaf tea.

Part of her wanted to join Wes at his next assignment and see Dina again. She had been one of the last to melt away from Emmy's circle of friends. No, that was the wrong way of looking at it. Emmy may have considered herself the victim back then, but almost a decade later, she knew better. The fault was hers. Dina and a few others tried pulling her back in, made a concerted effort to reverse Emmy's tailspin and help her through the dark times. They didn't know until a few months later what it was about, and by then she'd turned vitriolic, cruel. Dina had a kind heart, but her patience only went so far. Emmy understood, didn't hold a grudge. She was never the victim.

If there was a victim in all of this, it was Gabe.

She sipped her tea and smiled. Gabe, with his bushy black hair and dimpled smile. He could have had any girl, but for most of high school, he focused on Emmy. She liked the attention and the attention it garnered from the girls in her class. But at a certain point, it wasn't enough. Life came at them fast. Choices—short- and long-term—and Emmy was tired of making the same ones, or having them made for her, the dutiful kind that parents boasted about: being good, making curfew, cramming for tests, and having those little calluses form on your hand from no. 2 pencils. What was the point? She wanted to have a little fun was all. Or at least that's what she told herself. And Gabe was just a reminder of all that was chaining her to a life she didn't want, as well as most of her friends. And her clothes. She was determined to set out on her own.

When she went to break up with him, Gabe's look almost changed her mind. Almost. She saw his dimples, the ones he used so well to flirt with, contort in pain. She hadn't put much thought into her speech, most of her attention then was on getting it over with, but when she saw the tears, it finally dawned on her that he was crushed. No one had ever crushed him. She'd rationalized that they were still in high school, it wasn't a big deal, he'd be dating someone else in college anyway. But Gabe hadn't thought that way, at least not at the time. And maybe he never did.

Emmy managed a few sips of tea before pouring the rest down the drain. She shuffled back into her bedroom and turned on the light to her closet. This time Baxter didn't stir. Dogs had some kind of internal clock that told them when to expect a walk, and since this wasn't it, he didn't bother perking his head.

Emmy rose on her tiptoes and pulled a small shoe box off the top shelf. Inside were pictures from high school—the good years. There was also a letter from Gabe, the last one he wrote her, after their breakup, when she thought she was on her way to a mountaintop and didn't see the cliff she was about to jump off of.

> Emmy,
>
> I'm not sure what it is that you are going through, but I want you to know that I love you. Still do, always will. You can pierce your nose and dye your hair and change from sneakers to those weird Goth things I see you walking around in, but you'll always be Emmy to me. Yeah, I'm hurt you dumped me. I'm hurt I may see you with some other guy—even more undeserving than I am. But I can get over that. I just can't shake the feeling you need someone to talk to but you're not going to speak up until it's too late. Don't do that, OK? I'm always here for you. Always. Just, whenever you need me, call.

Emmy folded the letter and gently put it back into the shoe box. There were at least a dozen letters in the box from Gabe. Most of them love letters, and she used to pull those out when she needed a smile. His tone was always soft, comforting. That was Gabe. A perfect personality for a doctor. If that was what he ended up doing with his life.

She could almost recite the letter from memory. "Just, whenever you need me, call." She glanced at her iPhone, charging on the nightstand. How wonderful it would be to call him, to hear his voice.

Then she shook her head and put the lid back on the shoe box full of memories.

Chapter 18

Emmy leaned on the nurses' desk in the middle of the ER floor in the middle of her twelve-hour shift. She and her colleague Sue glanced at the room four doors to their right. The patient's chart lay on the desk for a nurse to pick up. Neither budged.

"I can't believe triage let him in," Sue said.

"We're a hospital ER, so we can't kick him out," Emmy said. "Kinda goes with the territory of saving people from the jaws of death."

"Yeah, but come on. His story doesn't match his 'symptoms.' Back pain? He was walking fine when he came in. What do you think the odds are he's a drug seeker"

Emmy glanced at the ceiling like she was calculating percentages in her head. "Seventy-five." She took the chart and looked over the notes made from the triage nurse. "More like ninety . . . Well, time to save another from the jaws of phantom ailments."

The number of malcontents who walked through the ER doors bothered her. People with lung cancer who snuck out of their rooms to the smoking area outside the hospital to light one up. Men and women complaining of chest pains who, fifteen minutes later, were banging on the vending machine for a bag of Doritos or a candy bar. Parents with crying babies in their arms who had the latest smart phone and a pack of cigarettes in their pocket but said they couldn't buy infant Tylenol.

Their conditions were one thing; their attitudes were quite another.

She'd been warned in nursing school that the people she would treat in the ER wouldn't always appreciate the care.

The worst were the drug seekers.

Emmy knocked on the door to room 113, then poked her head around the curtain. She looked the twentysomething male over. Bloodshot eyes, no surprise. Faded Kid Rock T-shirt and jeans, sneakers so grimy she couldn't recognize the brand. Fidgety, scratching his forearms. When he looked at Emmy, she saw in his eyes he was already working on a story.

"So what seems to be the problem?" she asked.

"I've got the worst migraine of my life," he began, pointing to his head as if Emmy wouldn't know where headaches occurred. "I think it started when I was lifting boxes at my cousin's apartment. I hurt my back."

"Have you taken any Tylenol? Motrin?"

"Nah, I'm allergic."

"To what?"

"Them."

"Both?"

He shook his head but didn't meet Emmy's gaze.

"So you threw your back out, and it gave you a headache?"

"It's crazy," he said. "I know all you nurses is so busy, so I don't want to take up too much time. Could you just give me a prescription to help with the pain, and I'll be on my way?"

A sweet-talker, Emmy thought. Most of the drug seekers usually were. She'd almost rather have patients frothing from the mouth and upset at their condition than have patients conjuring up crises. "I don't think that's the problem," she said.

"You gotta treat me," he pleaded. "I ain't feeling good, and I need to feel good so I can go to work tomorrow to support my momma and daddy. They ain't well neither and need me to pay for groceries once a week."

He'd moved on to the sympathy card. Emmy didn't respond—instead wrote notes in his file. The patient leaned forward, trying to see what she wrote.

"I wouldn't," said Emmy without looking up. "You might hurt your back again, remember?"

He leaned back and stayed perfectly still, like a dog waiting for a treat.

Emmy closed the file. She held it next to her chest as she addressed him. "You know what this looks like, right?"

"I'm in pain and I need treatment and you have to treat me."

"We haven't seen you before," she continued. "That's actually working to your advantage. Usually by now I would have called security. Almost all of the nurses in this hospital would have called security. We've got a roomful of sick and hurting people, and you just proved to me that you aren't one of them."

The color drained from his face. He leaned over toward the chair in the corner and snatched his coat in nervous excitement, then realized he hadn't played up the back injury again. Emmy watched as he cursed himself under his breath. "If you don't give me what I need, I'll just go to another hospital," he said. "It ain't right, what you're doing, not giving me medicine. I *am* sick, lady."

"Hold on a second," Emmy said. She pointed her phone at him.

"What are you doing? Did you just take my picture?"

"And sent it to all the surrounding hospitals. There's an app for that. Your picture's on their triage desk now, so I wouldn't recommend going anywhere else. And it'll be forwarded to the local physician offices by tomorrow morning."

"You can't do that."

"Sit down," Emmy said. She knew how and when to put enough authority in her voice. She doubted he saw that coming from a female; most men with bad attitudes and phantom illnesses didn't. But if she could order a first sergeant with a leg wound to stop fidgeting and pay attention so she could sew stitches and get him back to his squad, Mr. Drug Seeker was a walk in the park. He sat.

"Let me explain something to you," Emmy said. "We get drug seekers in here every day of the week. Occasionally they filter through the cracks, but most of the time we catch them. And there can be legal consequences.

Do you know how many people are allergic to all of the over-the-counter medicines but just fine and dandy with morphine or prescription drugs? Try practically none."

"Don't call the cops, okay? I'll leave."

"Not yet. I'm not calling the police on one condition." She handed him a card. "It's a good clinic for folks who are having a hard time with prescription meds and drugs."

The man tried to hand the card back. "Don't have no drug problem."

"You're a twenty-four-year-old man who walked into an ER and lied about a bad back and a headache," Emmy said. He nodded and pocketed the card. "Go see them. It doesn't cost much . . . it may not cost anything at all. And it's worth more to you than anything you're trying to get by lying your way into a hospital room."

Sue met Emmy at the nurses' desk. "You let him walk out of here? Without calling security or the police?"

"He wasn't a threat to anyone but himself."

"He'll just go to another hospital."

Emmy laughed and told Sue about the photographs.

"You can really do that? Send pictures of these guys to other hospitals?"

"Of course not! Major HIPPA violation. Illegal and impossible. But so was what he was doing. I didn't even take a picture of him. I pressed a button on my YouTube files to make a noise, then e-mailed a file to Wes."

Her phone rang. As if on cue, Wes was on the other line. She hadn't talked to him since yesterday's basketball game and was just about to answer when the ER doors burst open, chaos flooding in.

★   ★   ★

Emmy crashed on the cot in the supply room as the adrenaline faded. Her shift had ended an hour ago, but she hadn't finished treating patients until now. She worked the last few hours over and over in her head, wondering if there was a way to fix what had gone wrong. Not with the patient—with the relatives. And no, she knew there wasn't a way to amend it. What was broken was broken and needed time to mend.

A car accident. Bad one. Two teenagers in a car. The driver had been texting.

The passenger was the worst of the two—severe trauma to the head and plenty of broken bones. She'd been life-flighted from the scene to Emory in Atlanta. The driver was unconscious when the ambulance arrived. Broken nose, cracked ribs, a banged up knee, and lacerations—but he'd live. And walk, with a little rehabilitation. It was when they got him stabilized that the chaos ensued.

The parents of both teens arrived at the ER at different times and in ranging degrees of distress. The parents of the girl should have driven to Atlanta immediately, but they didn't. They waited in the Talking Creek ER to confront the driver's parents and tried to bully their way into the driver's recovery room to give him a piece of their mind. They were angry, and they let everyone around them know it.

"My daughter could be in a coma because of Nate!" the father shouted, while his wife sobbed uncontrollably by his side.

"Easy, Mitch," the father of the driver said, his hands up in defense.

"No!" Mitch's face was red, contorted.

"Sir, your daughter is being life-flighted to Emory," Emmy intervened. "You should—"

"He was texting, wasn't he?" Mitch asked. "Texting and didn't look where he was going. That stupid son of yours and that stupid convertible you gave him. We knew it was a mistake for Mandy to go to the movies with him and his low-life friends."

"Hey—" The driver's dad began to defend his son. But Mitch brought his shoulder around to land a punch.

Emmy had taken action. She hooked her arm around Mitch's elbow and used his force against him, slamming him to the ground. It took her and the security guard to pin him down. His eyes were wild, bulging.

"I'll sue!" he said. "I'm going to sue you all!"

Emmy put both hands on his face to make him look at her. "Sir," she said in a calm but authoritative voice. "We could throw you in jail, the way you are acting. I don't want to do that. It's a traumatic situation, and you need to remove yourself from here. Go. Drive down to be with your daughter."

"Come on, Mitch," the mother said, her arm extended, and they retreated into the parking lot.

Emmy took the elevator to the second floor and walked to the driver's recovery room. His parents had left momentarily to collect some things at home for an overnight stay. She poked her head around the door and saw the charge nurse checking his vitals.

"Is she gonna make it?" the boy in the bed asked.

"What's your name?"

"Nate Stroud."

Emmy shuddered. Nate Stroud, Talking Creek's starting shooting guard and All-Region selection his junior year. Yesterday she sat in the stands watching what would turn out to be his last basketball game of the season. Maybe ever.

"It's nice to meet you, Nate Stroud."

"Mandy—is she gonna make it?"

Emmy exchanged glances with the charge nurse, who finished her work and left the room. Emmy approached Nate's bed.

"She was life-flighted to Emory in Atlanta. She's in bad shape."

Nate stifled a moan. "I could die."

Emmy could see the despair in his eyes. She'd had the same look too, years ago. His pain started to take Emmy down a road she was all too familiar with, but she forced those thoughts away and focused on Nate. "You'll make a full recovery with some hard work rehabbing."

"All I did was look down," he said. "Friends texted, said they'd be a few minutes late. I was gonna heckle them because they're always late. I didn't see the light turn red; it wasn't even yellow when I looked down."

"You should get some rest."

"It should be me in that helicopter. Take a girl out for a date and look what happens. I wish I was dead." His voice cracked. "Just go," he whispered.

"I'll check in on you tomorrow, Nate," Emmy said, and closed the door behind her.

Chapter 19

On Saturday, Talking Creek's girls team didn't muster much of a game with Canton High School, but everyone in attendance knew why. Mandy Summers was still in critical condition at Emory.

Wes waited after the game to talk with Canton coach Dina Bowman, the usual postgame questions. But there was another reason he wanted to talk with Dina—her childhood connection with Emmy.

The more Wes thought about it, the more he realized he didn't know all that much about Emmy's high school and childhood days. He knew bits and pieces. She had lived in Athens all her life until college. She kept in touch with fellow soldiers and relatives. Her aunt Lynn was also in that circle, and instrumental in Emmy moving to Talking Creek.

From there, though, the lifelong locks associated with living in one place all one's life weren't there. The pictures in her apartment were of her, Wes, Lynn, and her niece Addy, and scenes and people from her tour in Iraq. Maybe a couple from college and Rome. Nothing from high school. He'd never met an acquaintance from Athens, never overheard her talking on the phone with a childhood friend or seen her e-mail one. There had to be at least a few living in the Atlanta area—Dina, for instance. Why hadn't they connected? Talking Creek wasn't far from Canton. Should he be concerned? Wes didn't know.

The locker-room door opened, and Dina stepped out in a business suit.

"Coach Bowman," Wes said. "Contributor for the *North Georgia News*. Have a few questions about the game if you've got a couple of minutes."

He clicked on his digital recorder and fired away. Dina's team had won 56–45. He asked about zone presses, her leading scorer, and their record in regional play. Dina answered his questions with her arms folded.

Wes gave his best impression of an interested listener, but in truth he was eagerly awaiting his next line of questions. When their discussion wound down, he turned off the recorder, signaling an end to being on the record. "I wanted to ask you something not related to the game, if I could. Do you know Emmy Stewart?"

Dina's arms unfolded. "Wow, that's a name from the past. Yes, I do. We went to school together. Why?"

"I know her too," Wes said. His cheeks reddened. "We're dating, sorry. I guess I just feel sheepish about saying stuff like that."

"We grew up together," Dina said. "We went to the same church and youth group. We both loved playing sports. She was into soccer. If she had stuck with it, I bet she could have gotten a scholarship. So how is she doing?"

"Great, great. You haven't spoken to her in a while, I take it?"

Dina nodded. "Not in a long while. I heard she went to Iraq and back. Truthfully, I don't think she's spoken to too many people from our high school class in a while. I doubt she'll be coming to the reunion next year. You know, after the whole Gabe thing."

A rock dropped somewhere in Wes's stomach. Dina read it on his face. "Did you not know about that?"

"Uh . . . I know some about Gabe, but I haven't met him."

"I can't believe she hasn't told you. Look, I think you should ask her about Gabe. I don't think it is my place with you two dating to say anything. Just ask her, okay?"

Chapter 20

The temperature was pleasant for mid-February—a verifiable heat wave in the 50s—but uncertainty cast a chill. Wes lobbed a tennis ball high into the air. It landed like a dud only ten feet from where he and Emmy sat on a park bench.

"That was an awful throw," Emmy said.

Baxter was busy sniffing the fringes of the chain-link fence enclosing the dog park. "I don't think your dog is interested anyway," Wes said. "So I'm in charge of this guy for three weeks when you go off to your training?"

"Afraid so."

Wes didn't want to admit it, but being in charge of Baxter was kind of comforting. It at least showed that Emmy trusted him with something while she was away. She could have asked her parents, Lynn, or another relative or friend. Wes could have viewed it as a consolation prize, but watching Emmy run beside her dog, he knew that wasn't the case.

"Don't worry about fetch," Emmy said. "He'll get his exercise. As soon as he starts chasing a smaller dog or has one of those Labradors on his tail. I want to hear what your mom told you."

Wes told her about his grandmother and dialysis, and his mom's prognosis and need for a transplant. How he'd already started research on transplants and how to try and expedite the process. Emmy listened patiently.

Wes shook his head in frustration. "We've got family up there, which is why she moved, but I'm her son—I don't like her being so far away while this is going on."

"Most people don't expect or want treatment for something, but it happens," Emmy said, and she told him about Nate Stroud and his girlfriend, Mandy Summers.

"What a tragedy," he said. "Good kids and good parents, aside from the whole attempted-assault thing."

"Sometimes you have to let those slide," Emmy said. "The Summers got a break though—Mandy's condition has improved. But it's going to be a long recovery for both of them, especially for her."

Wes shook his head. "I don't know how you do it."

"Treat people in the ER?"

"All of it," Wes said. "How do you deal with broken bodies and families? How did you cope with the soldiers you treated in Iraq?"

"Hour by hour," Emmy admitted. "But I had a choice. I could either be scared of the unknown or be hopeful. Scared a terrorist would put a bomb along the road to the hospital or hopeful we'd get to the wounded in time to save a life. When you replace fear with hope, you've got a chance."

"You and my mom—eternal optimists."

"There's worse things."

At the far corner of the dog park, Emmy and Wes could hear the howl of a beagle. A few seconds later, Baxter came around the small bend that had shielded their field of vision. He was on to a scent, but soon lost track as one of the Labradors crashed into him. Baxter let out a deep-throated bark at the collision. The Labrador paused, then dug in his paws and lunged at Baxter. The chase was on.

"Look at the little guy go!" They laughed as Baxter ran circles around the bigger dog, until the Labrador gave up and began pursuit of a larger, much slower, dog.

"It won't be boring with him. I can tell," Wes said. "I'll probably take him on an installment of the Civil War tour. We're going to Pickett's Mill in Cobb County when you're gone. Going to Cass next weekend. Should be fun."

"You mean Baxter is going to meet Ron before I do?" Emmy punched him in the arm. "That's not fair. You know I want to meet him."

"When you get back, how's that?"

"Deal," Emmy said.

"From your deployment."

Emmy wound up for another punch, but Wes deflected it. They watched Baxter run himself into exhaustion before he retreated to the public water bowl, where he slurped a few times.

When they got back in Emmy's Cherokee, Wes decided to speak over Baxter's panting noises. "Emmy, yesterday at the basketball game in Canton, I talked with Dina Bowman."

"What did she say?" Emmy sounded neither excited nor worried.

"Well, at first we talked about her team, seeing as they whooped Talking Creek."

"Not surprising," she said. "Canton's always had a strong team, and she was one of the best. I'm happy to see her succeed as a coach."

"We talked about you too," Wes continued. "She told me to ask you about Gabe."

Emmy's eyes narrowed. "What did she tell you?"

"Nothing," Wes said. "She said it'd be better if I asked you. Which is what I'm doing."

Emmy's gaze lifted ever so slightly, which didn't give Wes a warm, fuzzy feeling about where their conversation was about to go. But he knew they needed to have this talk.

"You already know that we dated in high school," Emmy began. "It didn't end well."

"Did he hurt you?"

"Nothing like that."

"Did you two—go too fast?"

Emmy shook her head. She let out a breath of frustration. "He was my high school sweetheart, Wes, but no, we didn't do anything regrettable. Not together. I got into some things I shouldn't have halfway through high school. I rebelled. And part of that rebellion was dumping Gabe. He still cared about me and had feelings for me and tried to help, but I was pretty mean to him."

How did all that relate to Emmy now? "So—do you still have feelings for him?"

Emmy pulled into the closest parking lot and turned off the engine. "Do you trust me?"

"Yeah, I guess." He corrected himself when he saw the look on Emmy's face. "Yes, I do trust you."

"I love you, Wes," she said. "I've loved two men in my life—you and Gabe. I loved Gabe because he was a great guy and treated me wonderfully, and I regret what happened, but you don't have to think like that about him. It's not like that."

"Emmy, I don't know *what* it's like if you won't tell me exactly what it *is*."

"I will when I'm ready." She started the engine again. "For now, all you need to know is you and I are together. And what's in my past, I may think about it, but it doesn't have the bearing you think it does on us. And I will tell you everything when I get back."

"From your training or deployment?"

"Training. Deal?"

"Ouch, put me in a corner there, huh?"

"Deal?" Emmy repeated.

"Deal."

Chapter 21

Wes surveyed the inside of Ron's F-250: the plush leather seats with seat warmers, satellite radio, four-wheel drive. Pretty much all the bells and whistles you could cram into a vehicle. "Nice ride," he said, thinking of the economical Camry he'd left in Talking Creek.

"Not as fast as a Corvette, but worth the trouble, right?" Ron wore a proud smile and sat in the driver's seat as if it were a throne.

"I bet the payments are more than your rent." Wes felt thankful he hadn't been to Ron's apartment. Something about seeing where Ron lived didn't sit well with him.

Ron chuckled. "Just about. Always wanted a big truck, just never had the money for it."

"Even when you were supposed to be paying child support?" The words spilled out.

Ron didn't act hurt. "I didn't have money back then, period," Ron said. "I wish I had—paid child support, that is. Spent some time in jail for that too. Your mom thought I should, seeing as my daddy was a big shot VP. But he spent more than he made, and when he and Mom passed, there wasn't an inheritance as much as debt. Old beat-up truck of his was about the only thing I inherited. And you turned eighteen a long time before that happened. Then I got my act together, and instead of getting a bigger place, I got an extended cab. Don't regret the decision one bit. This big rig is here to help."

Ron dialed his satellite radio to a comedy station, and the two listened to some rural Mississippi comedian recounting a trip to the big city of Chicago. The act lasted long enough for them to get off I-75 and over to Cassville, which was less town than post office and railroad tracks. Waiting for them near a stop sign and three markers was Paul Gavin and a handful of students.

"He don't look happy with us," Ron said. Wes checked his watch: five minutes late. The undergrads, it seemed, got a grace period not afforded to the lone graduate student.

Paul nodded as if their presence allowed him to begin. "What we have here, ladies and gentlemen, is the last best hope of General Joseph Johnston and his Confederate army of turning Sherman and giving him battle during the Atlanta Campaign. It's here that Johnston chose to make a stand. He planned to destroy a column of Sherman's fragmented army before reinforcements could arrive. And it almost worked."

"All I see is a stop sign and three markers," Ron said, hands in his pockets.

Paul frowned. "It is difficult to picture the past when asphalt and modern buildings have sprouted up over what used to be a dusty road and a handful of farms. It's the same in Atlanta; downtown where there are pricey restaurants and office buildings there used to be massive fortifications." He pointed northward. "But picture for a moment twenty thousand soldiers over there, waiting to spring an ambush for the approaching Union corps."

"Why didn't it work?" a student asked.

"The human element, of course. And chance. Johnston sent John Bell Hood, his eventual successor, to wait for the Union column. But Hood's men made contact with another Union outfit—cavalry—and he mistook that for a much-larger force and withdrew. There was a lot of finger-pointing in generals' memoirs in the years to come as to who should shoulder the blame."

"Sounds like one of those court shows on daytime TV," Ron said. "Not that I watch those. Much. I don't watch them much."

"Right," Paul said. "On that note, does anyone have any more comments or questions before I continue?"

★   ★   ★

With the history lesson over, Paul suggested lunch at a BBQ restaurant off Highway 41 in Cartersville for anyone wanting to stick around. None of the undergrads took him up on the offer, Brownie points completed with the tour stop. But Ron slapped Paul on the back like it was the best idea he'd ever heard.

Wes looked at Paul as if to say "I know what you're up to," but Paul didn't blush from playing the role of sage advisor. He led the way in his SUV while the Watkins boys followed.

When their food came, Wes lazily picked at his chicken salad and watched Ron slop on what looked like a double order of pulled pork and french fries while Paul approached his BBQ sandwich with the slow precision of a chess player.

Halfway through the meal, Paul looked up. "So, Wes, how are you juggling work and school and your other responsibilities?" He pressed his napkin to his lips as if he were more interested in cleaning BBQ smudges than posing the question.

Wes glanced at Ron, who continued to work hard on the pulled pork. "Fine I guess."

"Even with your trips to Nashville?"

Wes looked at his professor, eyes direct. He had confided in Paul about his mom—his concern for her and her need for a transplant. He'd been looking for prayer and advice from another believer. But now Paul was obviously suggesting he tell Ron about Janet? What business was that of Ron's? Or Paul's? The whole situation—Paul asking Wes to bring his father along for the tours, the letters, and now lunch—was beginning to grate.

"I'm fine. Just grading papers and writing and rewriting term paper proposals."

Ron snorted between bites and tapped Wes's shoulder with a hand smeared with sauce. Wes gave his father a dirty look and wiped off the sauce. Then he looked at Paul again to see if he wanted to continue.

Paul met his gaze and nodded in surrender. The table was silent until Ron scraped the last of the baked beans off his plate.

"Been a pleasure, boys, but I have some business to attend to," he said. "Need to get Wes back to his place and me to my apartment."

"Business?" Wes asked.

Ron grinned. "My buddy Otis and I wanted to do some car scouring up near Blue Ridge. Seeing as you don't have an interest in classic cars, and I do, and Otis does, well, we like to go kick some tires around old lots when we get the chance. It's good for the soul. Ain't nothing wrong with a little engine-revving therapy."

Chapter 22

Even during the weekend, the rehab center looked like a high-tech fitness club. Patients in varying degrees of recovery were working their bodies, trying to regain the ability to stand, walk, grip a pencil, or toss a ball.

Emmy spotted Lynn working with Nate, a little over a week removed from his car accident. Rather, Lynn standing by Nate, who sat on a mat like a kid in time-out.

When Lynn saw Emmy, she elbowed her off to the side. "Won't even stretch," Lynn said. "We haven't even gotten to the hard stuff yet. He's not responding well."

"Maybe if I talk to him."

"Be my guest."

Nate feigned indifference by looking out the windows to the parking lot.

"Mind if I sit?" Nate didn't answer, so Emmy sat. "You'll recover quicker if you do what they ask you to do, you know."

"Hurts."

"Broken bones and ripped muscles will do that. It'll take time, but the important thing is to get up and try and push yourself every day."

"Why?"

"Because your body—"

"You're not listening," Nate snapped. "Why should I bother?"

"Do you want to be crippled?"

"I don't want to be anything. I don't want to be here or have Mandy in a hospital bed or know her parents are wanting to press charges with the cops. I just want to be left alone."

"You want it to go back to the way it was," Emmy said. "Won't happen. Do you think Mandy would like that you're sulking?"

"Don't bring her into this."

"Why not? If you need a starting point, thinking of her is a pretty good one, because you're not doing you or her any favors whining."

"Who do you—"

"I'm a combat medic, and I've seen worse get better," Emmy cut in. "At the aid station in Iraq, we had these two soldiers come in. They'd been clearing a house and some explosions went off outside. Couldn't sort who was who, gunfire was coming in from insurgents. Somehow these two guys, best friends from all accounts, ended up shooting each other. One had some bones fractured in his right leg that would heal over time; the other needed his right leg amputated. We stabilized them both, side by side, before they were flown to a hospital in Baghdad. I remembered their names and tracked them down when my tour was up. They'd shot each other, but who do you think felt worse?"

"The one who shot his friend's leg off."

"Right. But a funny thing happened. The amputee wasn't angry. He knew the risks. He knew he was just as likely to be the one with the fractures. Mistakes happen all the time, and when they happen in combat situations, you're going to be wounded or worse. So when they returned stateside, the amputee kept on his friend, didn't let him sulk about what happened. He was there for every rehab appointment, and the two worked their way back side by side. They were from the same county, so they both became volunteer firefighters. A little after a year of being back, the soldier with all the guilt ended up saving two children from a burning house fire. He won a civic award and accommodation from the county. Two kids—alive because of him."

"Some other firefighter would have saved them if he didn't."

"You don't know for sure," Emmy said. "I know of dozens of stories like that. What kind of person is Mandy? Is she mean? Does she hold grudges?"

"No, she's the exact opposite."

"Then why do you think she'd turn on you? We're all the bad guy at some point in our lives, Nate. It doesn't mean everyone gives up on us. A few will. But not everybody. And the ones who stick with you can give you hope that the rest will come around. Don't sell yourself short on Mandy."

Chapter 23

When Wes opened the door, the first thing he noticed was the smell. The one-bedroom apartment stunk of sweat. On the lamp stand to the right of the hand-me-down sofa was a deodorizer, but it couldn't absorb all of the odor. Not pungent, just a noticeable trace of a blue-collar man who didn't have a woman around to tidy up the place or hose it down with potpourri.

The TV was an old clunker. Wes surmised that one of Ron's clients had given up on it and Ron had hoisted it into his truck and nursed it back to health. A huge bookshelf housed dozens of DVDs, CDs, and one row of paperbacks. A video-game console sat on the floor, as did an assortment of electronics in various stages of repair. Wes pictured Ron playing Halo or Madden online with a teenager from Ohio, and on another day he would have laughed.

This apartment was his father's life. On a shelf, Wes saw one faded picture of himself when he was a one-year old and a picture of Ron with some buddies. Most boys grew up wanting to be like their fathers; Wes had prayed for the opposite. He wanted a steady paycheck, career path, and the love of a woman he'd never let go. Emmy might be that woman, and if so, Wes promised himself he wouldn't go down a dark, deserted path that led to a place like this.

Wes always wondered if Ron's genes would lead to his own life's collapse. Thus far he'd kept his mistakes few and stayed out of the trouble Ron had gotten into. Still, could he destroy his own life like Ron had?

Could he make such terrible choices he'd end up living alone, on the wrong side of town in Marietta, working on appliances with the future as dim as the light coming in from the lone, grimy window?

Wes took a deep breath, reminding himself that Ron's phone message had been urgent and slurred. Despite his misgivings, Wes knew he had to hear what Ron had to say.

"I'm glad you came, son," Ron said, patting Wes on the shoulder. Wes balled his fists only briefly, but he couldn't think of any other way to help absorb the word *son*. References to their relationship made him uneasy, especially now.

Ron's eyes were bloodshot. Stubble sprouted from his chin. His oily hair sprouted out of his head like weeds. But worst of all was the familiar smell.

"Makers Mark, or Jack Daniels?" Wes asked with an edge in his voice.

Ron's eyes opened a little wider in recognition of the slight. An alcoholic being accused of another drink. But he was guilty—they both knew it—and he merely lowered his head and nodded.

"Five years, down the drain." Ron shivered as if the realization chilled his body. "I'm sorry, son."

There it was again. Son. How could this man call him a son when he hadn't done any parenting to qualify? He was a certified mess, not a father. Wes fought back the urge to poison the room with hateful words. *Deadbeat, loser,* he wanted to say. He'd expected this, eventually. He'd sensed deep down that their peaceful trips to the Civil War battlefields would lead back to this. Wes swallowed the anger in a long, deep gulp.

"Besides the drinking, and most of my life you wasted by not being around, is there something more specific you're apologizing for?" Wes asked.

Ron nodded grimly, and limped to his sofa, favoring his left leg. Wes sat in the easy chair across the room. It creaked like one side was about to give out, and he shifted his weight just in case.

"I messed up," Ron said. "Big-time."

"How? Be more specific."

"I drove out of state."

"I'm not following."

"I can't drive out of state without permission," Ron said. "Parole officer says I can't. And I did, Otis and I, but I was driving. I didn't think it would be a big deal, except I wasn't planning on getting in a car accident. Some lady in a minivan ran through a stop sign and sideswiped my truck."

"Why were you out of—"

"Doesn't really matter, because that traffic accident forced my hand. I left the scene. Imagine that. The one time where I'm the victim and I hightail it out of there. I was going to take the truck to the shop yesterday morning, when my parole officer paid me a visit. I didn't want it any worse than I'd already made it. I 'fessed up. Long story short, son, I'm probably going back to jail for a while."

This was the man he'd known as a child. Reckless. Stupid. Always making the wrong decisions. Sober and coherent, he'd been almost likeable. But he was reverting to his old self.

"Don't look at me like that," Ron said, watching Wes clench and unclench his fists. "I didn't bring you over so you could yell at me. I just thought you should know, hear the story from me and not the papers or a phone call from jail."

"When did the drinking start?"

"After the parole officer left," Ron said. "Nice man. He didn't like reporting it. But the law's the law."

"And you know how to break it."

"Everything seemed up, you know? You and me, we're talking. I'm not drinking. I've had a steady job for a while. It's good, honest work, and I'm doing the kind of work God created me for. I've been clean for five years."

"Past tense," Wes said.

"Do you have to dig like that?" Ron asked, almost pleading. "Stop looking at me like I was running drugs or out to shoot someone."

"Were you? You and Otis doing something you weren't supposed to?"

"I didn't do anything to anybody except myself. Otis ain't in no trouble."

"Otis who? What's his last name?"

"Spencer. Why?"

"From where?"

"Coweta County. I didn't know him from jail, if that's what you're asking."

"You said you both like cars. Isn't that what got you into jail in the first place, breaking stolen cars down in a chop shop?"

Ron shook his head. "It's not like that. My reckoning's been made, all right? I'm gonna have to go back to a place I swore I'd never return to." He looked to the ceiling. "Lord, forgive me. I am so sorry I went down that path again."

Wes watched as Ron buried his head in his arms and sobbed. For a moment, Wes pitied him. If they'd been close, he pictured himself patting Ron on the shoulder or even giving him a hug. But they weren't close, not even a little.

"I need to ask a favor," Ron said. He raised his left foot. "I got so tore up and mad last night, I kicked a hole in the wall. I think I broke some toes. Can you drive me to the clinic? And then to the hardware store? I'll get the drywall and plaster and patch it up, but I don't think I can drive today."

Wes had seen someone kick a hole in a wall once. A high school sophomore during a basketball tournament. The kid went for an easy layup on a fast break and missed. In frustration, he'd kicked a hole in his rival's gymnasium wall and created an instant news story for Wes. "Eagles to foot bill for player's foot attack on rival gym."

This was different. His father still acted like a teenager. Had Ron stayed out of jail and off the drugs and maybe, just maybe, controlled his alcohol consumption, there was still this. His arrest record was riddled with as many bad choices as the chemicals he ingested. And that was the problem.

They could never be father and son. Wes was the responsible one, the mature one. He was embarrassed by what Ron was and what he did to himself. Wes didn't know if Ron could ever shake it, or if he wanted to.

"I don't think I can drive you," he lied. "I've got a work assignment to finish. Maybe you should take the bus or something."

"Can you help me up, then?"

"Not until you give me a straight answer on everything," Wes said. He turned and walked out the door.

On the ride home, Wes simmered over his father's stupidity. Maybe it was worse because he'd begun to trust him. Whatever. He determined to pitch the rest of Ron's letters and be done with the man.

Once home, he made a beeline for his desk with letters piled in two stacks—both his father's and copies of Benjamin Watkins's. He rushed so fast into the room that he sent both stacks flying. Groaning, he began to sort through the letters to throw Ron's away. But his eyes settled on one particular letter. He hadn't opened it yet, but today he unfolded the letter and read the first line. It was almost an apology for now, almost like Ron had realized that even if he and Wes spoke again, they'd return to this point in their relationship.

He sat down on the floor and read the letter.

Chapter 24

I won't tell you everything, just what you ought to know. I didn't plan on any of this, even after the arrest. But life got tougher, like a bolt tightening. I served a month in the county jail and spent three months picking up trash on the highway, curbs, and anywhere else the state told me to. I lost my job trucking soda across Atlanta. I sold my truck because we needed the money. The owner of the appliance repair shop kept me on, but the pinch we felt in the wallet was now like a grip that'd make you want to cry uncle. Your mom and I, we were both exhausted, and put what little energy we had into you and not our marriage. Both knew it was just a matter of time.

I can't give you much as far as fatherly advice, but a road map to purgatory or worse? Yeah, I've got that in the glove box. I did what I thought I had to do, what I thought needed to be done. Let me tell you something—when your insides are burning, you can darn near justify anything. When the water shuts off and the heat won't come on until you pay the gas company, and people won't hire you because of a smudge you made being frustrated with your lot in the first place, you start looking at things differently.

It started innocently enough. In jail I met this grease monkey from Acworth named Darrell—he was in for drug possession or something like that. We chatted up cars and engines to pass the time. He said when we both got out, there was a shop owner he knew, could get me a part-time gig. I'd wanted to own a car shop for the longest time, had promised my daddy I'd go through college first, earn a business degree, swore on that used Corvette he bought me. But considering he sold it for gambling debts, and I dropped out of college, and we needed to keep the water running and power moving, why not?

Didn't take me long to figure out he was running a chop shop. I'd come by in the morning, cars would be waiting inside the pitch-black shed, never outside. We'd toss out license plates, do paint jobs and new tires and just enough to give it a new identity, and then he'd roll it out to whatever guy he had lined up to sell 'em off. Or we'd just scrap a car and sell the parts. But he paid, real good, and I was in a fix.

I could blame Darrell for getting me into the drugs, but that'd be excusing myself from a fate I would have met regardless. I'd drink, smoke, snort, whatever it took to get away from my problems. I hid the drugs from your mom, first out of shame, then out of practicality, so I wouldn't run out. You want to know when your marriage is in trouble? When you stop fighting.

One night, the papers landed in my lap. At first I didn't know what they were. Your mom had dropped them from above the couch. I spilled whiskey on my left knee. She wasn't going to discuss it, and I don't blame her. All she wanted to know was if you were tucked in, if I had brushed your teeth, done anything remotely resembling parenting. You were asleep, but you'd already learned to fend for yourself when I was at home.

By that point I realized what the papers were for—divorce. I flung them off my lap like they were a coiled rattlesnake. She folded her arms and said she couldn't have drugs in her child's house anymore, couldn't have an apathetic, criminal father . . . that she'd go it alone if she had to.

I should have sobered up right there. Sworn off the drinking and smoking and car chopping and everything. But I didn't. I took another sip for courage, raised my glass in the air, and proposed a toast, that she finally got something right. Told her she'd made plenty of mistakes too, and she would again, and she'd come calling for me.

Tears formed on the edges of your mother's eyes, but I didn't have any comfort in me. I marched into the bedroom and slammed the door. I grabbed a suitcase in the closet and threw clothes into it. Outside the room I could hear cries—both from your mom and from you. Sometimes you were scared of monsters under the bed or in the closet.

I was the monster. Reconciliation crossed my mind. Counseling, therapy, whatever it took. Even divorce and just trying to be the best father I could be, despite my shortcomings. But would that take the dull ache away from my body? The emptiness? No, nothing could. And maybe your mother was right. Maybe I wasn't cut out for the family life. Maybe those feelings of wanting a fresh start could finally be realized. They'd all be better for it, I thought, as I listened to my son scream.

I opened the bedroom door, picked up the divorce papers, crammed them under my arm, and walked out on you and your mom.

Chapter 25

At the beginning of the week, Wes learned his father would be packing for jail—again. At the end, Wes sat on a large cardboard box and reviewed his life. The surroundings were fitting. While most families piled, stacked, and tossed their memories into the confines of a garage, basement, or series of closets, Wes and his mom had packed them into a storage unit along a busy, four-lane road in Roswell, Georgia.

They'd settled on this storage unit because of its other means of revenue: rented trucks. While most teenagers had used their first weeks and months with minted driver's licenses cruising around town with friends and dates, Wes had hopped into a moving truck and braced the highway to help Janet move. Even if the law had said Wes should wait a couple of years for that responsibility, his mom had considered him up to the task. So perhaps he did have memories associated with this place.

He breathed in the musty air and pondered how to transfer the boxes from this storage unit into his waiting U-Haul truck and drive it north to Tennessee.

Surprisingly, after a whirlwind January, February had slowed to a crawl. Cooled was more like it, following Ron's painful reminder. But things were gaining momentum heading into March. Wes had just enough time to drop off the load in Nashville, get a good night's sleep, then turn around and drive home in time to get Baxter from Emmy before she left for training. It was taxing, trying to keep up with everyone else's lives and possessions, but somehow it comforted Wes to know he was trusted with so many things . . . and by different people.

Surveying the size of the unit and comparing that to the size of the truck, Wes thought he'd have enough room to clear everything in one trip. He silently thanked his mom for being a neat freak. She'd marked every box clearly and made a path down the middle so everything in the shed was easily accessible.

He worked his way up and down each row of boxes. Interspersed with his mother's keepsakes were some of his own: "Wes's College." "Wes's High School." "Wes's Middle School." He noticed two from his grade school days and then turned to see one labeled "Baby Pictures."

Methodically, he cleared out the storage room, moving the boxes with his name to the side until they were the only ones remaining. Now was as good a time as any for a break, so he went back to the truck for some water and a snack. He chewed on a granola bar and scanned the box labels again like titles at a record store, looking for a starting point. Baby Pictures. He pulled out what was clearly a baby album, stuffed full of pictures of his first days on earth. In this world and its snapshots, Wes had two parents who loved him and apparently loved each other. Wes stared at the pictures of Janet and Ron hugging each other and Janet with Wes in her arms, Ron huddled over, pride in his eyes. The scene was surreal.

"How'd we get from there to here?" he said aloud. His voice echoed around the empty shed. He turned the page and studied a large picture of him and Ron, a close-up. Ron's face was flush with happiness. Wes had pictured Ron sitting in the waiting room with dread, but in these photos Ron embraced fatherhood.

Wes thumbed through the rest of the album. A copy of his birth certificate was in the middle of the album for some reason, but the rest of the pictures were positioned chronologically. He worked his way through his first accomplishments: smiling, rolling over, sitting up—Mom had gotten them all on film, and Ron was featured in most of the events.

Wes finished the last page of his baby book and moved on to other albums. As he grew—graduated from diapers to undies, small boots to bikes—his father's presence waned in the visual stories. Ron was present for Wes's third birthday, but somehow absent from his fourth. He was there for Wes's first day of school but absent for the tooth fairy. The family albums confirmed his first memories—of a drifting, absentee father whose presence faded away like print on old newspaper.

The pictures registered Ron's deteriorating frame and pale face from late nights at the bar, raising Wes's memories of booze on his father's lips. He sniffed the air and could almost smell it again. He noticed on a page full of pictures of their trip to Allatoona that a picture was missing at the top. He'd have to ask his mom why.

The album from his grade school days was the last one he would look at. There wasn't much else to see after that. His parents had already split and his mother hadn't taken any pictures during the few visits Ron made. From fifth grade on, it was Wes and his mom and occasionally her relatives.

He felt like he'd just watched a movie where you hope at the critical moment the characters will drive down the right road and avoid trouble, but of course that wasn't the case. His parents' fate had been trapped and recorded in these photos, and there was nothing he could do to change it.

Wes picked up the baby album again and returned to the large picture of him and his father. He studied Ron, his expression, and realized after a few moments his fingers were tapping the page as if he was thumping the man.

"I don't get it," he said. "You're happy here. You've got it made. A beautiful wife and a baby boy. And then you go and trash it, just throw it all away and only look back long enough to remind me what an absolute failure you were. Are. How are you even my father? You can barely keep the power company from turning off the electricity."

Wes felt the heaviness set in, the burden it was to be asked to forgive Ron. He set down the baby album when he realized tears were forming. He cupped his hands to pray, but he didn't know what to say or who he was praying for—himself or his father. No inspiration came, and he wasn't sure he wanted any. The last time he'd really, truly prayed, it was to figure out whether or not to call Ron, and look how that turned out.

Wes wiped his eyes and took a deep breath. As he leaned over to pick up the baby album and put it back in the box, he noticed that crammed behind his birth certificate were two pieces of paper. Curious, he pulled them out, studied them. Documents. The type was faded and the inked signatures even more so. Yet that wasn't the reason he read them three times.

He couldn't believe the documents existed in the first place.

Chapter 26

Emmy had dozed off on the sofa watching a romantic comedy. She often did this before training, cramming as many cheesy TV shows or movies into her time off as possible, then working off the junk food and pizza out in the field, where calories burned away like ammunition from a submachine gun. What she didn't have was Wes, who was off playing mama's boy by delivering a U-Haul full of boxes to her today in Nashville. More and more she realized how much she'd miss him while deployed.

It was a new feeling—having someone to come back to instead of something to run away from. Her first deployment, she used the long hours and high stress to ward off the ghosts, who couldn't haunt in unfamiliar places. It was true that combat changed you, but for Emmy it was a welcome change. She was no longer an adolescent. She was a combat veteran, in more ways than one. But now, with Wes, she was entertaining the role of spouse . . . if he still had the ring when she got back from Afghanistan. Maybe after she returned from training and her yearly self-inflicted trip to Athens, she and Wes could talk. About a lot of things.

The phone rang from what seemed like the other room. She shook off her grogginess and reached over Baxter. The caller ID said Wes.

"Hey," she said. "I was just thinking about you. Are you in Tennessee yet?" She could hear the rent-a-truck bouncing along the highway.

"I'm heading up there now. Listen, I need your advice. I don't want to say specifics but I'm working some things out after this morning. If you found out a horrible thing about someone you loved, what would you do?"

Emmy's stomach turned. Was he talking about her? *No, he couldn't be,* she thought. *How would he know?*

"What horrible thing?" she said. She wasn't ready to talk, not yet. "Who is this about?"

"I just need to know," Wes said. "I mean when you've spent all the time you've known that person and then you find out they aren't who they said they are—at all—what would you do?"

"Is this about me?"

Wes paused. "No," he said. "Should it be?"

Emmy had never heard that tone coming from Wes. She'd never been insulted or hurt by him, but the lack of emotion in the question threw up red flags.

"I don't like where you're going with this," she said. "You're scaring me."

"I'm sorry," he said, more like the Wes she knew. "I'm angry, but not at you. I'm going to have a really long and painful talk with someone."

"Are you looking for advice or an excuse to go ahead with whatever argument you've already put into your head?"

"Okay, Emmy. I'm trying to calm down."

"At least don't call whoever it is you're mad at; that'd be cruel."

"I'm actually going to drive right up to her doorstep in about an hour. It's my mom."

Emmy waited for more. "Do you want to tell me what happened?"

As she listened to the story, a hint of guilt crept in. She wasn't so forthcoming with her past. This was a sensitive subject for Wes, ever since she'd known him. But she had watched his progress with his father, trying to create an open dialogue. Ron had jeopardized that, and now Wes had discovered something even more jolting.

"I feel like I read one story all my life," he said, "and now I'm finding out there were missing pieces. Inaccurate interviews. For the longest time I believed her story that Ron had an affair and that they divorced because of the affair and the drug abuse. Ron told me awhile back he didn't have an affair—I thought he was lying. But was he? How much of Mom's story was true? I don't know if I can trust her—and that's awful, because she was always the one person I could trust. The only one."

"Are you mad enough to confront her today?" Emmy asked. She wondered how he would react when he found out about Gabe. Would he be upset? It'd change a lot about their relationship and his perception of her. Should she tell him now? No, she needed the time at Fort Gordon to work out what she'd say. The training, the trip back to Athens—then they'd move forward. Wes had enough to deal with right now.

A pause. "I don't want to confront her at all. I don't want to ask her and see her dance around the subject, not with her health going downhill. But this hurts."

"Then pray."

"Pray?"

"Yes, pray. Whatever it is that's tearing at you, pray. Give it to God."

"He's had it all along, you know," Wes said, an edge in his voice that Emmy didn't like. "That's what I was doing before I discovered this, actually. Not sure if he's the best source of counsel."

"Listen to yourself," Emmy said. "You're working up some anger at God *and* your mom? Is it worth that kind of trouble?"

"Probably not," Wes said, sighing. "I can't help it. I mean she should have told me. I can't believe, all this time . . ."

Emmy realized she was looking at the problem from the opposite perspective. Maybe Wes realized it too. She hoped he did, although she wasn't ready to tell him why.

"Look, even if you're mad at everybody, pray, okay? Take a deep breath, and then when you are ready to confront her, do it calmly. Don't even think of it as a confrontation. You're a reporter collecting facts. Think of questions that could ease you into the talk without cornering her. Just don't bring a digital recorder into her house, might scare her."

"You're something else, you know that?"

"I'm glad you said that."

"Why, you like positive reinforcement?"

"No," Emmy said, exhaling in relief. "You came back from the ledge. I needed to hear it."

"Well, I don't like this any more than you do. And whatever happens, it's probably going to be bad. But I'll give patience a try."

"And that means there is hope," Emmy said.

For you and for me, she wanted to say.

Chapter 27

When Wes signed the contract for his first job out of college as a sports reporter for the *North Georgia News*, in the back of his mind he thought maybe, just possibly, it'd be the first step to a career as an investigative journalist. Sure, the sports stories of northwest Georgia athletics weren't scandalous. A football coach in Ellijay took a last-minute offer in South Georgia that left his team high and dry before two-a-days, and a blue-chip recruit switched commitments from Auburn to Tennessee on signing day, but there wasn't much in the way of scandal, and by the end of his tenure, he didn't have the same enthusiasm to look for one.

When he left the paper and started freelancing, he thought the itch was effectively scratched. He'd moved on to the next one, grad school. But was it normal for a guy in his twenties to be watching press conferences on CSPAN and CNN for the questions and not the answers? He got a kick out of watching a presidential press secretary get grilled on some quote his boss made a decade earlier to a labor union, or the CEO of a major oil company defending profits and explaining green initiatives. And the drama coming out of athletes' mouths—a mix of third-person pontifications and outright absurd cutdowns of opposition? Wes often left the sports station on for those stories.

But he wasn't enjoying this. Not one bit.

He wondered for the first time if his anger toward Ron was misplaced. Apparently his mother had some secrets of her own. Had she kept Ron out of Wes's life for so long to keep that secret from him?

No, that didn't make sense. If Ron wanted to tell him, there were ample opportunities. A phone call or chance meeting. Mom hadn't screened Ron's letters. Ron hadn't brought up the subject during their Civil War trips. He hadn't even used it limping around his apartment, pleading with Wes to drive him to a doctor.

The vision of his father's outstretched hand froze in his mind like a judge's gavel about to strike. He tried to convince himself as he drove to Nashville that if only his mom had given him the truth, he would have done the right thing and taken Ron to see a doctor, despite the booze on his breath. Who knows? They might have already reconciled long ago. His mother's inability to face her past continued to torment his present.

He kept repeating that line of thinking, but it wouldn't stick. He didn't want to let out the questions that were filling his mind like a plugged sink. He didn't want to ask a question, have her evade it, and see the deceit. Not from his mom. But he did want answers, even if they were painful. What would happen after that, he didn't know. In some ways it wasn't up to him.

"How was the trip?" Janet asked. She held out her arms for a hug, but Wes hurried inside with a box.

"Is something wrong?"

"Where do you want this?"

She eyed the box's labeling, then Wes. "Are you sure you're fine?"

"Just tired," Wes said. Of what, he didn't offer. "Where do you want this?"

Mom directed him to the guest bedroom. And that was how most of the afternoon went. Wes and Janet emptied the rental truck, and she told him where the boxes should go. When he was almost finished, she left a plate on the kitchen counter with a sandwich and orange juice. Wes took it and sat down without thanking her.

"I saw that there's one more box in the truck," she said. "Do you want me to get it?"

"Sure. There were some old photos I wanted to take back with me, but we can sift through the box to see what stays and what I can take back."

He'd left it there as a test, open, with his baby book at the top and part of the incriminating documents sticking out.

Janet pulled out the baby book and waved it at Wes when she returned. "Guess who looked adorable when he was a baby?" she said

Wes stopped eating his sandwich and stared at his smiling mom. The edges of the album were clear, its contents tucked neatly inside. He put his sandwich back on the plate. "I had some questions, actually, about that period of time."

"What would you like to know?"

"Tell me about your pregnancy."

"Just to fill in the blanks?"

Wes swallowed a lump in his throat. "Yeah. Didn't see any pictures of you being pregnant."

He watched as his mother answered. "It was a crazy time, what with both Ron and me in college. I don't think either of us owned a camera, and we weren't around our families much. Ron went out and bought one with what little money we had when you were born."

"So, no pictures because of the—unplanned—part of the pregnancy."

Mom tilted her neck. "Yes, but we adjusted. I think we more than made up for it with pictures of you from newborn to one. Ron worked two jobs to help pay for our place and school."

"And you stayed in school."

"I went back after a semester off. Our plan had been for me to graduate and then him return."

"Now we've got plans."

"I don't like the tone in your voice."

"I'm sorry," Wes said. "You know, I was looking through the album before I loaded up the truck. There's something missing. A picture."

She remained stoic. "Oh?"

"Yeah," he said. He sat beside her and flipped to the page with the missing photo. "First spot on this page, seems like a photo was ripped out."

She nodded. "Your father took that. When I gave him the divorce papers, he left abruptly. Later he came back to get some things and asked if he could keep one picture. I thought it would be one of just him and you, but it was all of us, standing in front of the truck in the Allatoona parking lot."

"I was at his apartment and didn't see it," Wes said. He shut the album in one quick motion. "Whatever happened to the truck?"

"He sold it. Last good thing he did. Sold it because he lost a job after going to jail. It helped pay for a few bills. He held it over my head too—like I didn't have to make any tough decisions and was looking for an easy way out."

Wes handed her his glass. "Would you mind getting me some more OJ?" She took the glass and headed for the kitchen.

Alone in the room, Wes opened the album. The documents were gone.

Chapter 28

Paul had seen the look many times. Cold eyes, attentive in a methodical sort of way to a certain task, but distant, tending to an emotion deep within. Shoulders tight, hands still when they shouldn't be, as if the man's body was so taut from a decision he was going to burst. He'd settled those nerves on Hueys coming back from a Vietcong ambush where a young platoon leader had lost his heavy weapons squad, and on Northwest Georgia football fields when his all-American quarterback son fumed over a left tackle missing a block. He'd measured men and boys, found ways to reach and pull the warmth back into their eyes, the reason.

This, though, he wasn't sure how to approach.

"I'd like to give my presentation on what Benjamin Watkins thought of the generals leading the war," Wes said in a rehearsed voice. "The inspiration for this came after your presentation at Cass, where General Johnson concocted a counteroffensive that ultimately failed due to bad timing and execution. By this point in the Atlanta Campaign, Benjamin Watkins was troubled by the retreat."

Paul nodded for Wes to continue, and Wes began to read Benjamin's words:

> I do not know why we cede land so easily. Surely we
> could have made a stand at Cass or Dalton or a dozen
> other well-suited places north of here, but instead have given

precious ground before Sherman as if we were welcoming him into Atlanta.

I pray for our leaders, but do they know best? Surely they have more reports, more rumors and gossip to sift through than I could comprehend. Yet I can't help but wonder what a Lee or even the Union's Grant would do in these circumstances differently than our Johnson. It seems only weeks ago we enjoyed high morale and fresh rations in Dalton, ready for a fight. Now we've run to Atlanta, and I wonder if I'll be running home to you soon, the retreat so far on.

Wes pulled out five history books one by one from his bag, biographies of generals and thick accounts of the western theater of the Civil War.

"You've thought a lot about this," Paul said. "Weren't you visiting your mom this weekend? You must have been up all Sunday."

Wes cringed at the mention of his mom. "I've been leaning toward this direction for a couple weeks. This weekend's study just . . . solidified it." Paul watched as Wes shook off whatever emotions tried to weigh him down and continued. "I just think it would be a good contrast—comparing the leaders who made decisions that affected their soldiers and then the soldiers who suffered for it."

Suffered. Paul studied Wes's face, flat, unmoving. Something had happened recently, since their visit to Cass—maybe between him and his father. Paul had been disappointed in that trip—had hoped for Wes to share with Ron that Janet was sick—but perhaps he'd rushed things. Lately he found himself studying his conversations with Wes like a commander studies a topographical map.

Wes wasn't Michael. Paul knew that, but when the opportunity had presented itself, literally at the moment he was about to turn in a piece of paper signaling his retirement, how could he pass it up? Wes had come into his office with the idea of those letters, the same letters Paul had seen Ron and Michael talking about a few years back.

Wasn't Michael's last wish connected to Wes's family? To show him the power of grace and forgiveness, how it can permeate and then overwhelm even the worst of conditions? He'd seen the impact Michael's story had on Wes. Wes had witnessed grace, but applying it was a different matter.

There were two conversations here. On the surface, a discussion about a research paper. But below the surface, Wes was struggling with something, and Paul wanted to find out what it was. He glanced out the window at the tall oaks and considered his next words.

"Mr. Watkins," he began in his professorial voice, "history is saturated with such what-ifs that Benjamin speaks of. Our founding fathers were originally thinking protest, not independence, when the British rolled out a new level of taxation. They adapted to the changing temperament of the colonies. I could list several Civil War battles that turned on random chance—individuals capitalizing on unforeseen opportunity—including Cass. Often, some of the most important speeches were given on the fly. Think of Roosevelt reacting to Pearl Harbor or Cronkite to the death of JFK. Their words cut to the collective conscious of their audience."

Paul put his elbows on his desk. "All of that said, I don't think you have finished your thought. This is much better than your original proposal, as it delves into Benjamin's state of mind, deeper than dates and places on a map, but what is the outcome? How does Benjamin come to grips with the shattered campaign, or does he? How does he and every other soldier feel about their state of affairs? This isn't so much about the leaders as it is about fortune and how each man deals with what he can and cannot control. Perhaps a look at the parables would shed some light on the subject."

"The parables?"

"Is something else on your mind? There's an edge to you today. It's none of my business if you don't want to share, but has something happened between you and Ron?"

Wes gripped one of the history books tight. "You mean besides him violating his parole? Getting drunk and then calling me? No, even that's not it, actually."

Paul fought to keep his shock beneath his facial expression. He wondered if reuniting Ron and Wes, making such an effort to accelerate things, had been a mistake. He watched as Wes stirred in his seat, clenched his fist, and shook his head.

"You'd think that would be enough," Wes said. "Ron is a deadbeat; I've known that pretty much all my life. But I found paperwork in an old album when I was loading up boxes in Janet's storage place to bring them up to her. Hidden behind my birth certificate were papers from the state and an adoption agency. Her signature was on both forms. Apparently she'd signed her rights away as a parent; she just never gave me away."

"Wes, I am sorry," Paul said.

"Is there a parable for this?" Wes asked. His eyes filled with tears. "I know the prodigal son bit. But what if your parents are the prodigals? Or one's the prodigal and the other's left a lie hiding behind your birth certificate?"

"I'm at a loss," Paul said. And for the first time in a long time, he felt helpless, worthless.

Wes quietly gathered his books and papers and clamped his bag shut before slinging it over his shoulder. His voice sounded tired, dead. "I'll have another proposal for you soon, Professor." And with that he quietly closed the door behind him.

Chapter 29

G<small>et</small> down!"

Emmy obeyed the order even though she didn't see who issued it. She flung herself against the dusty Humvee's back wheel and made her body small. Around her, boots kicked dirt as soldiers looked for cover and others returned fire. She hugged her knees as she looked not thirty feet in front of her. A gunner with a .50 cal machine gun had gotten into the fight.

The gunner's target lay on the other side of the vehicle, so he rotated the massive gun toward Emmy and began firing. Emmy plugged her ears. The sound coming from the gun was devastating, and so too would be the trail left behind by the rounds—if they were live ammunition. Had Emmy been the focus of the gunner, she and the vehicle she was crouched against wouldn't be in one piece following the barrage.

"Clear!" an officer boomed.

Emmy's unit had been attacked by insurgents posing as civilians. They'd come to the checkpoint with a story of a wounded child, and once they'd lured in a soldier, the insurgents brought out assault rifles and grenades concealed in the back seat. The battle had been short—Emmy was impressed with how quickly her unit responded and put the enemy down. But it came with calculated wounds and casualties—laser targets on each soldier for simulation, or one of the instructors pointing to a soldier and saying "Dead."

Although these sorts of simulations were planned to sharpen the skills of combatants, Emmy used it to prepare herself for the chaos of a battle-field. She surveyed the losses: three wounded soldiers, one "dead" from her unit; four "dead," one wounded of the insurgents. Soldiers closed in on the remaining insurgent cautiously. A pair of soldiers knelt down to the "dead" enemy to check for weapons. Emmy's eyes went wide as she saw one of the soldiers begin to flip one of the "bodies" over.

"Check for grenades!" she screamed.

But it was too late. One of the instructors tapped the soldier on the shoulder. "Dead," he said. "The insurgent was wired with a grenade to go off when you turned him over." He looked at Emmy and a soldier nearby. "You and you, you're wounded."

Emmy mumbled her frustration under her breath and headed back to the Humvee. She flipped her helmet off in disgust and pulled at her hair to untangle a knot. The other "wounded" soldier stood beside her. "Hey, it's just training, right?" he tried to joke as he took a gulp from his canteen. "We'll be patched up in no time and back out there."

"No use to us if we don't take this seriously," she said. "And if this was a real fight, you wouldn't have a medic to treat you, because I'd probably have a leg blown off, and Sergeant Foster over there would be full of lead and KIA."

Emmy uncapped her canteen and chased her frustration with three large gulps of water. It was March, which should have meant cool temperatures, but she was in full "battle rattle" like everyone else, and with her smallish frame, she needed to stay hydrated to keep going. She made it a point to be her company's nagging mother, reminding soldiers to stay hydrated or become casualties.

In two months it'd be the real deal, she thought. She looked at the make-shift town behind her, part of an artificial campaign on the grounds of Fort Gordon meant to get this unit combat ready. She thought about the base beyond, its soldiers and their families and how quiet these places could get when army units deployed. With the National Guard, it'd be more like fire stations, hospitals, engineer firms that would feel their absence.

In Afghanistan she would be part of an aid station; firefights like the one just simulated would mostly be miles away and the mess would be shipped to Emmy's station full of nurses and doctors. In the more chaotic battles, their job was to triage, stabilize, then call some birds in from the hospitals to transport the wounded who needed surgery. Unlike going outside the wire, her hours would be sporadic—boring in some cases, impossibly frantic in others.

But, she reminded herself, she'd have a line back to the States. In Afghanistan there'd be barracks, calling cards and phones, probably Internet access, and possibly videoconferencing with family. That was more than she got at the makeshift station in Iraq. She'd be able to watch movies, eat fast food occasionally, and see Wes's face on Skype—which was important, because she was planning on asking if he would keep Baxter while she was deployed, so the two boys in her life would be in one spot.

She wondered if Wes had talked to his mom about the paperwork. The phone call on his way to Tennessee had startled her worse than some of the more stressful ER scenarios she'd come across. He'd returned to pick up Baxter earlier than anticipated, which wasn't a good sign.

But how *was* he supposed to act? What do you think when you find out you were almost put up for adoption? How do you deal with the nonevent? Wes was questioning how much else there was to his past that Janet erased and rewrote, about herself and about Ron, and Emmy didn't blame Wes for his doubts.

She had left for Fort Gordon with Wes's world upside down. A twinge of guilt crept in that she was the first domino in all of this, that she couldn't fill the void Janet created, because she too was holding back. But not much longer. Once the training was over, three weeks all told from the beginning of March, she'd get her visit over with, drive home to tell Wes, and be done with it. For another year, at least.

Chapter 30

A beat-up Nissan truck, smaller and older than Ron's, pulled into the Pickett's Mill visitor lot. Ron and Otis shook hands inside the truck's cabin and had a joke while Wes waited with Baxter beside him. When Ron stepped out, his smile evaporated. Otis nodded from the truck and pulled back onto the road that circled around the lot; then he disappeared around the bend of trees.

Ron put his hands in his pockets and closed the distance to his son. "That's a heavy face," he said. He reached down and petted Baxter.

"Got some questions," Wes said.

"Fire away."

"Let's walk first."

The Pickett's Mill battlefield consisted of a ravine surrounded by small fields and rolling hills and a small creek that lined the base of the land. With flowers in full bloom and the grassy slopes filling with color, the view from the top of the ravine was breathtaking. It was also the best observing point for what happened on the battlefield. Wes had already studied the highlights—how Sherman had bloated his supply wagons and jumped off the railroad route to try and flank the rebels in the high country, how rains slogged the roads and slowed his progress. Instead of making a flanking maneuver, the armies rolled along these hills fighting a bloody stalemate in a series of battles, the last ending here at Pickett's Mill, a battle Benjamin Watkins had fought in.

The battle was much like any Civil War engagement: if one side had arrived sooner and with more force, perhaps the outcome would have differed. But an attempted Union charge was foiled by an entrenched foe and confusing terrain. The main point of reference was the ravine he and Ron now were in front of. A brigade of Union troops had marched down into it and only a handful marched out—a spot ripe for killing. The Confederates had shredded the Union troops in a matter of minutes. They walked down the trail, Baxter weaving and bobbing with each fresh scent.

"Thanks for coming early," Wes said. "Let's talk about Otis. Do you know his background?"

"Yep."

"Convicted felon? Money laundering? Stolen *cars*?"

"In his past. He is a good man."

"Is he?"

"Yep."

"The stuff that got you in trouble, is that in your past?"

"You think I'm back on the sauce?"

"You were. Have you had a drink again?"

"No."

"Drugs?"

Ron shook his head.

"When were your last?"

"Drugs—eight years ago. Never again."

"When did you start?"

"We're going that far back?"

"We are."

Ron folded his arms. "I tried some before I met your mom, but it was nothing major, nothing I couldn't handle, at least I told myself. That was a mistake. Then I cleaned up so I could take care of you and your mom. And I did, for a while. It fell apart when I got arrested at that bar after work."

"Did you cheat on her?"

"Janet? No."

"I may actually believe you now. Abuse her?"

"Besides being a bad father and neglectful husband, no."

"Cheat her out of money?"

"I didn't pay child support when I didn't have the money, if that's what you're asking. We've been over this."

"But you've got that big fancy truck."

"I get it. You don't like big rigs."

"Why were you out of the state, with Otis? You're going to jail for it, might as well tell me."

"Cars," Ron said flatly.

Wes glared. "Stealing?"

"Nope. I was looking for one."

"What? The Corvette your dad bought you and then sold off to pay the gambling debts?"

"He's your grandfather, not just my dad," Ron said.

Wes shook his head. "You risked violating parole for a car. Unbelievable."

"Life's about risks and rewards, I suppose."

"And what's the reward? Another sentence?"

"I'll write," Ron said. "Every day, if you want me to."

"That's another thing," Wes said. "Those letters. You were making half-hearted attempts at them, and then all of a sudden—bam, like junk mail. Why'd you start?"

Ron shrugged. "I knew you liked stories. Was when I met Michael. Just a coincidence your first job ended up being in his town. Well, not a coincidence to him anyway. But you know how it is with the Gavins. They say things to get you thinking. He encouraged me to write to you, even if at first it was just to get events off my conscience, hold them somewhere else. Then I could work on forgiving myself. Maybe they'd help you understand why I failed."

"Well, don't be so hard on yourself," Wes said. "You both failed." He told Ron about the adoption paperwork and how Janet had taken it from the baby album and said nothing about it.

"Maybe she thought it was a good reminder of making a good choice?" Ron said. "She didn't give you up."

"Because you probably convinced her otherwise."

"Ain't no convincing with that woman," Ron said with a light chuckle. He kicked a couple of rocks in front of him. "She'll make up her mind on her own. Like she did with you. Best decision she never made, is what she told me."

"You're defending her?"

"Why not?"

"All this time, you weren't the bad guy she made you out to be."

"Yeah, I was. Am. I'm still the bad guy."

"How can you say that? You stopped her from handing me over to an adoption agency."

"And walked out on her a few years later. I walked out on you."

"But you're not what she made you out to be. I kept you at arm's length, and I shouldn't have."

"Why are you so eager to defend me now?"

"You don't want me to?"

"It's not right, Wes. I was a horrible dad. Your mom, she took care of you, and now you're talking like you're going to disown her. Are you that quick to turn?"

"I don't know what I'm going to do."

Ron sighed. "Son, if you listen to me for just one bit of advice, just one, get those ears perked up good right now. You need to get this out of your system—all the hate and bitterness. It's eating you up. It'll turn you inside out and into something you don't want. It's as nasty as that ravine right there, where all those bluecoats died. It will swallow you up whole, like it did my life, if you don't get it in check."

Chapter 31

I read your story of Michael Gavin in the newspaper. I thought you captured the essence of Michael's life extremely well, probably better than I could have, and I've known him for a few years. So yeah, there's that. I want you to know that I didn't know about Michael's request. He'd encouraged me to reach out to you, even offered to be the intermediary, as if a guy you didn't know would persuade you to reconnect with me. But I said no, it wouldn't work.

If you're interested in knowing where we met, read on.

Prison, 2006. My world at that point was measured in inches. Nine feet, eight inches high, six feet wide, and eight feet long. Walls were thick cinderblock, cold to the touch. Light was a bright fluorescent bulb, probably purchased from the lowest bidder. Toilet sat feet from where I slept. My door wasn't mine to open. Rather, the state of Georgia told me when I could leave and who could enter.

I read and worked out to pass the time. Had a handful of Sports Illustrated magazines from baseball season, even though it was the middle of December. About a dozen paperback thrillers—sci-fi, lawyers chasing down big corporations, espionage thrillers from the Cold War. One book I didn't open, didn't have the courage for was my Bible. It reminded me of who I was and why I was there, and I didn't want to be reminded of my wicked ways.

Then a visitor, a former all-American, walked into the reading room one day with his own Bible in one hand and compassion for me in the other. Before you start thinking I welcomed him with open arms and changed my ways, don't. The sight of him repulsed me. Clean cut, in shape, life put together. Married. He was everything I wasn't, or so I thought. For some reason I'd brought the Bible out with me to the reading room instead of a novel. Wanted it to run away, get a life so it'd stop tormenting me. Attracted him like a moth to a summer lantern.

"It's a living, breathing thing." First words out of his mouth. I looked a little closer at this former football player and soldier and saw some frayed edges—strong arms built for labor, an Airborne tattoo that probably went along with a tour of duty, a scar on his forehead. He'd lived with fears, death, and struggle. His eyes said it and his mouth told. And he'd gotten out. I was at least curious to hear his pitch.

"It's in here," Michael said. "The testaments are chock-full of desperate men propped up by the Holy Spirit. Peter? He was a self-righteous, quick-tempered fisherman. Jesus made him the rock of his church. Saul? He was the early church's biggest enemy. Jesus had a little talking-to with him on the road to Damascus. You know what happened? He righted his wrongs, became a new man—Paul. Most influential missionary ever."

"I ain't no missionary," I told him. "Just an addict and a thief, bad one at that. You're something I could never be."

It wasn't the first time someone had visited the jail and told a sob story about problems with booze or drugs and how, gosh golly, he'd beaten it, and with a twelve-step program and a bunch of self-help books, maybe you had a chance too. I used their brochures for napkins and sometimes toilet paper.

What they never said, and what I always reminded them if they forced me to speak, was it's possible to beat drunkenness and drug addiction when you have a family that loves you and a wife to go home to and a kid who looks at you like you're his hero. Without them, the percentages dropped. Mine was at zero. Any chance for redemption died years ago.

Michael dropped his Bible on the plastic table with a thud. He stared at me like he was thinking of a locker combination. I gestured at him to proceed. "It's either you or a Wheel of Fortune rerun," I said. "I just bought you a couple letters. Spin."

He showed me some verses. "See this? Jesus is talking to a tax collector. See here, he's talking to the weak and the maimed. See this, he's on the cross with criminals—you and me—offering them the kingdom. He's got his Daddy's keys to the car and he wants nothing more than to take a road trip with us, my man. You believe that?"

"I believe those men aren't me," I said. "You ain't me either."

Michael closed the pages and put his hands on the table. "What do you want when you get out of here?"

"Do I look like the 'Seven Habits of Highly Effective People' to you? You're wasting your time, and mine. What does it matter? I lost everything. Marriage, my boy—all done and gone for because I'm a screw-up. That's what you won't hear from half of these inmates. Ain't their fault they're in here, yada yada yada. Well, I'm speaking it loud and clear. I started out a college student and ended up in a penitentiary because it all got too hard. What do I want? Not to screw up. That's what I want."

"That's not a plan; that's a prayer," Michael said.

"Then pray it for me, Mr. All-American," I told him. I was so angry I slapped his Bible to the ground. Guards shifted, began to approach us, and I was ready for a baton to the noggin, but Michael waved them off.

"Look, I get what you're trying," I said, trying to calm myself. "And maybe one day I'll start listening. But right now the only thing that book of yours means to me is a reminder of how awful I am and how awful I got it. Don't need reminding of that, see? Ain't no church going to take me in."

"Only the best ones, Ron," Michael said. "And I'll leave you with this. Comes time for you and the Lord to have a talk, it'll be right there in his Word, and it ain't a conversation anyone else needs to be around or have for you. Before you have a plan, you have to help yourself, heal yourself, then settle up. Just remember that."

Michael tore off a page from the back of his Bible and scribbled his address and phone number. I couldn't believe it—a Bible thumper tearing off a page from his own book. "If you ever want to talk about things, send me a letter. Or call. I'd be happy to stop by."

He did, a bunch of times.

That night, I looked across the cell at my Bible like it was looking back at me. I thought of bringing a picture of someone, but why have a picture of your ex-wife? Or your deceased parents, who would be disappointed if they were still breathing? Or the friends that didn't get you into drugs but didn't help you out? Or the friends that did introduce you to their good buddies Mary Jane or Crack or LSD, and yeah, why don't you fellas hang out for a while, but no, we'd rather not help you out if you two get into a lick of trouble. Or of you, all your potential walloped by a shaky father who couldn't keep himself out of jail.

Maybe you'd be the reason I'd finally get into the Word and the path this Gavin guy said led to some sort of salvation for a depraved soul. As I looked at the Bible though, I felt only guilt. Still, the wheels were in motion. Seems like Michael greeted us both where we needed him to, introduced us to who we needed to meet. Like father, like son.

Chapter 32

Wes sat in a chair in the corner of the patient room as Dr. Benewitz checked his mother's blood pressure. She'd already gotten her lab work in.

It felt strange to see someone else getting poked and prodded. Wes had been afraid of needles even before they discovered he had diabetes. He eventually grew out of it with the constant pricking and insulin. And right now the thought of a needle stick felt more comforting than working things out with his mom.

Even after a week to stew, Wes admitted that Ron was right about the anger eating away inside, and he wasn't happy about Ron being right about something. But as much as the adoption paperwork stung, his mom was his foundation. She wasn't exactly acting like she'd done anything wrong. Their greeting had been frosty, only slightly warmed by Baxter's antics to get a head scratch out of her before they put him in her fenced-in back yard for the afternoon, and Wes was starting to see her stubborn side. He didn't like it in her any more than the stubbornness he'd inherited. They'd agreed to focus on what ailed her body rather than their relationship while at the doctor's office.

"How is she, Doc?"

Dr. Benewitz smiled. "She's a fighter," he said. "But her creatine levels aren't where we'd like them to be, and they haven't been for a while."

"Anything on the transplant front?"

"No, I'm sorry to say. It's a long, long list in the Nashville area. And

133

unless she wants the offered donation, she won't be bumped up unless her condition worsens."

Wes's eyes raised. "Offered donation?"

Dr. Benewitz glanced uneasily at Janet and then down at his charts. He wasn't going to say anything further, Wes knew, without her approval.

"Mom?"

She looked at Wes and took in a deep breath. She nodded for Dr. Benewitz to speak.

"I had a man come to my office a few weeks ago. He said he wanted to be an anonymous donor for her kidney transplant. It was an unusual request, and of course it's only step one of a lengthy process to even see if he'd be a suitable donor. I had him fill out paperwork and asked him if I could disclose his name if she absolutely wanted to know, which of course, she did. Ron Watkins consented to this ahead of time and left a number where we could reach him. Currently your mother doesn't want to use that option in her treatment."

"Ron? How did he—"

Paul. Paul had told Ron about the kidney transplant. The reporter in Wes's mind was racing, connecting dots. "Ron crossed state lines to talk to your doctor, Mom. He got in an accident too. You've got to say yes!"

"This isn't your decision to make," his mother said.

Wes rose from his seat. "Doc, can you give us a few minutes?"

"I'm being as clear as I can," his mother said as Dr. Benewitz shut the door gently behind him. "The answer is no."

"Just like that, you've made up your mind?"

"I have. I made my decision when Dr. Benewitz informed me of the offer, and the answer is still no."

"He's going to jail because of this!" Wes said.

"I didn't know about that."

Wes took a deep breath. "He is trying to do something good here. It's your best option. This could save your life."

"I don't want to owe that man anything. Now he wants to swoop in like a hero? No thanks. Tell him when he pays up for all that delinquent child support, then we'll talk."

"Well, how about me?" Wes said, trying a different tactic. "I'm talking to you right now, aren't I? Mom, I found the paperwork in my baby album. I know about you wanting to give me away . . . and I'm here. We're not talking about you marrying him again. Just let him help you."

She didn't respond.

"Well?"

"I can't believe you'd use that against me."

"I'm not using anything against you. I just told you so you'd see that you can forgive somebody."

"Conditionally? You want me to take Ron's kidney so you'll find it in your heart to forgive me? You'll just bring it up again."

"Like you've brought up Ron's past? Like you told me he was having an affair but left out that he didn't start seeing that woman until after you were divorced? That they didn't meet until after you'd slapped divorce papers on him. Are you saying what Ron did has to be used against him at every turn, but you're clear?"

"I didn't do anything. You're punishing me for something I didn't do."

"How am I punishing you?"

"By trying to make me feel guilty. You want to use it as collateral so I will talk to Ron. I don't want to do that."

"Maybe you should feel guilty. Maybe that one pertinent piece of information would have helped me reconcile with my father. He wanted me when I came into this world, and you didn't, and there's paperwork to back that up."

"He won't go through with it. He'll find some way to mess it up and hurt me."

"How do you know that? How do you know he hasn't changed?"

"Did you know one night I caught him getting high? While you were sleeping in the next room, curled up with your blanket and crying, he was taking a hit. You could have rolled over and suffocated, and he wouldn't have known. He was stoned out of his mind on the couch watching late-night TV, and he thought you were a soda ad that wouldn't stop playing in the background! I will never, ever forget that night. I cleaned up your toys in the living room while flushing his drug stash down the toilet. I would not let a man like that back into your life as a father figure because he was barely ever a father. You can hate me all you want for what I *almost* did. But I'm not changing my mind."

"So you want me to forgive you, but you won't forgive him?"

"For a lifetime of me being your mother and providing for you, yes. It's different."

"It's the same!"

"Now you're sounding like Ron," she said. "Like father, like son."

He'd never had a conversation like this with his mother. What to say? He sat down in the chair and rubbed his knees. "You go to church and do the small-group thing and talk a big game about God and his forgiveness and grace, but when it comes time in your own life to forgive, you just can't."

"It's not that simple Wes."

"Yes, it is. You might have a kidney transplant in a much shorter amount of time and beat this thing. You have the chance to beat a disease that has killed and killed and killed in our family for generations. Or you can wait and let it continue to attack your body. Those cysts aren't going to call a truce on your kidneys. Your kidneys are shriveling. You may have to wait for years; you said it yourself. I just don't see how you can't take this and move on with your life."

"Wes, I will not accept that man's . . . token or gift or act or whatever it is . . . in order for you to love me, if that's what you're asking."

"I didn't say that. Look, just think about it, pray about it, okay?"

"I will pray."

There was an empty silence.

Dr. Benewitz knocked and came back in. "I went ahead and scheduled your first dialysis treatment, Janet."

Wes looked at his mom, pleading. She stayed focused on Dr. Benewitz. "Thank you, Doctor," she said. "I'm sure it'll help me feel a little bit better."

Chapter 33

Emmy tossed her duffel bag into the trunk of her Cherokee, flipped her sunglasses on, and checked her phone. Two messages—one from her parents and one from Wes, who had also left a text—a photo of Wes on his couch, Baxter sitting on his stomach looking up at the phone. She called him as she pulled out of the base and turned onto the road toward Athens.

"I'm glad you're coming back," Wes said. "You have no idea." They spent a few minutes catching up—Emmy telling him the number of times she was wounded in simulated combat, and Wes all of the parental discoveries.

"That's a lot to take in, with your mom and dad," Emmy said.

"Nothing compared to the babysitting. You'd better hurry. Your dog is eating me out of my house—including my deposit."

Emmy giggled. She could hear Baxter barking at something on the other end, in the low, guttural braying of a beagle. "It's good to hear your voice—and his."

"So when do you get back?"

"Can I ask you a huge favor?" Emmy said. "I want to go visit my folks. Can you take care of Baxter one more night?"

"Is something wrong?"

"No . . . just need a visit. I'll call you when I am on my way tomorrow morning, and you can come over, how does that sound?"

"I guess it will have to be okay. Drive careful."

Emmy tapped the side of her head against the window glass. She wasn't going to her parents', at least not initially. She could stop by for a minute later that night so she wouldn't be in a complete lie, but she was bothered with how quickly she'd thrown Wes off her trail. Still, she needed to do this one thing, get it out of the way, and then she'd be fine for a while longer.

★ ★ ★

Wes rubbed Baxter's neck. "So much for our little surprise." He looked at the decorations he'd placed around Emmy's apartment, as a test run for what he had planned for her deployment. Baxter wagged his tail on the floor and sprang onto the couch, nearly knocking Wes down.

"You act like a cat, and you're not. You're a thirty-six-pound beagle. You know this, right?"

Baxter put two paws on Wes and tried to lick his face. "I don't think I want a make-out session with a beagle on my girlfriend's couch, so let's go for a walk."

Wes grabbed his keys and the leash beside the door, prompting Baxter to do circles in the living room out of excitement. While he waited for the dog to calm down, he had another thought. "How about we go for a walk—then we have some flowers delivered to her parents' house?"

★ ★ ★

Emmy pulled off the loop around Athens. Where there used to be undeveloped land now stood fast-food restaurants, a hotel, and a motor-sports shop. The commercial side of Athens was spreading around the college town like kudzu. It wasn't until a few miles closer to the town itself and its neighborhoods that Emmy recognized her old haunts—shaded streets and sleepy roads. She passed the soccer fields where she'd spent so many of springs with grass-stained shin guards and a smile on her face.

She passed the movie theater where she had gotten her first kiss—freshman year, Gabe. She and Gabe told their parents they were going to see a comedy and instead snuck into an R-rated *Batman*. She remembered the butterflies from that sweet, brief kiss and Gabe's arm over her shoulder and then holding hands during lunch the next week at school as their public announcement of what had been obvious to everyone for years. Emmy and Gabe were soul mates. They'd be in the high school yearbook as "Best Couple," probably the first to marry and have kids. Their lives were charted before they'd even posed for their driver's license photos.

Emmy drove by her high school, within walking distance of the university, and suppressed the urge to lay low, as if her ghosts would come rushing out of the buildings and snatch her and hold her for all eternity, an example of failings to avoid. She wondered what would happen if she bumped into Mr. Reynolds, her English teacher, who'd pegged her as a sure-fire Rhodes Scholar, or Mrs. Featherly, the drama teacher, who'd thought she had such promise in her bit parts as a freshman. What did they think of her now?

She stopped at a red light. Her parents' house was three miles away, the only safe refuge for her in her hometown. Despite the havoc she'd created, her parents nursed her back to health, encouraged her. She drew strength from them to finish high school with courses at the community college so she wouldn't have to be on the high school campus. Her childhood home was like a foreign embassy in a hostile land, and she was tempted to just go have some of mom's potato casserole and drink coffee and argue politics with her father.

Three miles, to the right. When the light flashed green, she turned left.

★   ★   ★

Wes phoned Emmy's mom to tell her to expect the flowers. "Wanted to make sure the roses beat her to your house. When did she say that she'd be in?"

"She didn't. I wouldn't be surprised if she doesn't show up until tonight— or at all. She's been doing this for a while now. We know not to rush her."

"Rush her from what?"

"She comes home every year on this day. She's going to visit Gabe and his family."

"Oh." His heart sank. *Forget the flowers,* he thought. "Well, if she gets in, tell her to call me." But he didn't wait for a reply before he hung up. And he didn't expect a call from Emmy either.

It remained a pleasant neighborhood. The large brick entrance with bold letters greeted her. As did the clubhouse with the pool behind it where she'd spent many summer days playing, splashing, and eventually flirting with boys. The tennis courts, playground—all of it Emmy remembered fondly.

She took the first right, and her heart began to pound. She scrunched her fingers on the steering wheel and realized they were clammy. She wiped her left hand on her uniform but kept her eyes on the houses. She used each one like a countdown—four, three, two—until she came to the cul-de-sac. Then she began to sob. She could skip this part, she told herself. Drive right out of the neighborhood and straight to Gabe and the solace he provided her.

"Stop it!" she said aloud as she tried to collect herself.

Calm and collected Emmy. Steeled-emotions Emmy. Could get an IV going on a screaming child and pluck bullets from whimpering bar fighters. Not today. Today she wasn't an ER nurse or a combat medic. Today she was that teenager who showed up on the same doorstep after a nighttime full of mourning and prayers.

Chapter 34

"You know something I don't, don't you?" Wes stared at Baxter as if waiting for a reply. Baxter cocked his head.

Wes rubbed his temples with clenched fists. There it was. Emmy and Gabe. Whatever happened between those two wasn't finished. Apparently, each year they met and talked and didn't resolve whatever it was that needed resolving. Wes's thoughts went in directions he didn't like but couldn't control. *Did they have a baby? Were they married at one point? Was Gabe married? Were they still together?* He'd seen enough *Dateline* shows of husbands and wives leading double lives. Was that what was going on?

He glanced at Emmy's computer. A couple of hours ago he'd almost used it to order flowers for her. He had her passwords to e-mail accounts and bill pays and Facebook. She'd given them to him to check periodically during her training rotation as a sort of test for when she'd be deployed. Now all Wes could think about was using them to find out about Gabe.

It felt deceptive, but Emmy was being deceptive too.

Dig, said a voice inside him.

The fears simmered. His mom lied. His sweet, vulnerable mother hid a dark secret all those years. To know that his mother had considered not raising him, well, it hurt.

Dig.

But what did that have to do with Emmy? Nothing, Wes knew. Nothing, and everything. If he couldn't trust his own mother, how could he trust anyone? What did he build from now that his foundation had shifted?

Dig.

He logged on to Emmy's Facebook page and sifted through her friends list.

★   ★   ★

Emmy looked through the small garage window and saw two parked cars. Of course they were here. Where else would they be today? They were always here on this date, every year for ten years. She refrained from looking into the windows but visualized the inside of the house where she used to be welcome. Four bedrooms, three bathrooms, an upstairs study, and a finished basement where she played hide-and-seek as a grade schooler and spin the bottle as a middle schooler.

The mailbox identified the family with bold black letters: the Pattersons. Michelle Patterson had been a stay-at-home mom when Emmy was young. She always kept the neighborhood kids hydrated and fed. Michelle had driven Emmy back and forth to soccer practices too many times to count and even chaperoned some middle school dances. She was behind the punch bowl when her son Gabe nervously approached Emmy for the first time and they danced to the Boys II Men song "End of the Road." Such a sweet feeling of being wanted and loved, and Michelle had smiled in acceptance at them both.

Dan Patterson was a commercial real estate developer. He attended all of Gabe's baseball and football games and kept his son on a strict curfew that Emmy knew her own father appreciated very much. But Dan traveled a lot as well and wasn't always there to break up the mischief. It was in the Pattersons' basement as a fifteen-year-old that Emmy had taken her first sip of beer.

That led to her first can of beer, which led to a six-pack. She remembered the rush of drinking, despite what at the time was a bitter taste in her mouth. But that rush and excitement on something borderline innocent had led to a search for more rushes, more excitement, and ultimately crossed into more dangerous things.

The Pattersons poured all their love into their son's life—their youngest child. Gabe was the first on his block to own the newest, best video games. The Pattersons traded in his bikes more regularly for newer models and took him and his brother on Caribbean cruises and long summer road trips. He attended the best baseball camps—and for his sixteenth birthday he received keys to a brand-new convertible Mustang. Gabe was spoiled rotten but didn't act that way. His grades were good, and he was on track to attend Emory, like his father.

Emmy joked that once they graduated she'd have to break up with him—no self-respecting Southern woman and college football fan could date someone who went to a school without a real football team. He'd countered that they produced more doctors than UGA did NFL draft picks by a large margin, and she'd finish it by saying that who cares if you're a doctor if you can't throw a football ten yards.

Emmy smiled at the memory, but it quickly faded as she stepped onto the walkway, surrounded by flowers on either side. She'd never be used to knocking on the Pattersons' front door when she used to let herself in the back. But the front door signaled formality, and that's all her relationship with the Pattersons had become. Memories turned to formalities.

There was always hope. She said a prayer under her breath and knocked on the door.

Gabe didn't exist. At least not in Emmy's friends list. Wes was hopeful. It was normal for exes to blacklist each other after a breakup. He'd seen it a hundred times—someone going from "In a relationship" to "Single" in a matter of minutes. Pictures were deleted, messages nixed, portions of lives erased. That would explain some things but not all.

Wes clicked on her friends' Facebook pages. He simplified the search to Athens friends, including Dina. No one had a friend named Gabe or pictures of him. He closed out her Facebook account and rocked back in the chair. "This guy's got to be somewhere."

Dig.

He typed Emmy's e-mail password and searched her address list. Nothing. Then he filtered through old e-mails in her folders and finally did a search with the name *Gabe*. Nothing. He wasn't pleased with this kind of progress. Now Gabe was looking like a secret. Wes didn't know all the details because Emmy hadn't finished concocting an alibi, he reasoned.

Wes rose from the chair and walked a circuit in Emmy's living room. Emmy wasn't the kind of person to leave a diary. Of course, he didn't know that for sure.

Dig.

That's when a plan formed. He could rummage through her apartment and clean up before she returned. She was hours away, on the opposite side of Georgia. She'd never know. He could put on his investigative hat and turn Emmy's life upside down for clues and discover the secrets she wasn't willing to share.

Dig.

Wes looked down the hallway toward her bedroom. Maybe in the closet were pictures, letters, and remembrances of this Gabe guy.

If he did this, he'd be crossing the line. Well, he'd already crossed it. Emmy had lied to him. He wasn't lying, he was just . . . checking. He'd come clean when he found out what he needed to know. He walked into her closet, looking for the letters, and answers.

Chapter 35

Emmy was too tired to notice Wes's car parked between a motorcycle and minivan in the second row of her apartment complex. She fumbled with her keys and missed the "Welcome Home!" sign at the top of the doorway. She opened the door and missed the streamers and even larger "Welcome Home!" sign on the wall.

She did notice Baxter, who charged, hopped front legs first, and bounced off her side. Emmy wrapped her arms around him and buried her head in the fur of his neck, sobbing. Instinctively, Baxter stopped squirming and let her cry. When she looked up, she saw Wes sitting far to one side of her couch—and her box of Gabe's letters on the end table. She read his demeanor—not confrontational but not as warm and bubbly as their conversation the day before. And what was he doing here? He didn't move toward her.

"You know where I went," Emmy said.

Wes put his hands up. "No. I mean yes, but no, not really."

"Care to be more specific?"

Wes sighed as he mumbled for the right words. "I called your parents, and your mom said you might not even make it over there. You were going to Gabe's. She didn't say why, so I've got to ask. Why were you at your ex-boyfriend's house? And why doesn't he show up on Facebook or in your e-mail? Who is this guy?"

Emmy stared at him. "I was going to tell you when I got back."

"Well, you're back," Wes said. "All I need from you are a few details to fill in the blanks, because I stopped waiting. I'm a reporter. Well, used to be. And there's nothing against checking up on some things. Especially if my girlfriend won't tell me the truth."

Emmy remained silent. She leaned against the door and bit her lip.

"Look, I'm not mad," Wes said. "It explains a lot, you know, why you didn't want to talk about marriage or anything. You still have feelings for him and—"

"That's not it, I—"

"Let me finish. What else could it be? I should have asked more questions. That's my problem; I only see what I want to see. And with us, all I wanted to see was you and me and not anyone else, when there was *always* someone else. You've been struggling with it the entire time we've been together. You said you had a boyfriend and lost touch. Maybe he moved on, but you didn't. Is he married? Are you having an affair?"

"I didn't tell you everything, but I haven't lied to you," Emmy said, her eyes fixed on the floor.

"Yeah, I've been getting all kinds of that recently. No sugarcoating it, huh? Just tell me this: did I do something to deserve this?"

"Deserve?" Emmy shook her head. "We could have avoided all of this."

"Are you saying we shouldn't have dated? I—I think I need to leave," he said. "I don't want to say anything I'll regret, and boy am I close."

"Please stay. I need to tell you more."

"Didn't you already have your chance, every day? Why now?"

"Because none of it's what you think. I didn't tell you because I didn't want it to matter as much as it did. I didn't want my past to have anything to do with us. But it did—it does."

"Because you still have feelings for Gabe."

"Because he died—and I'm the reason."

★   ★   ★

Emmy had mulled over the words the last few months—in the shower, at work, driving to and from errands, even walking Baxter. Some days they encouraged her; she thought about the release the words could offer. She imagined saying her piece to Wes and having her burden lighten. It wouldn't completely go away, like when stitches were taken out but a scar remained. And the scar would still aggravate until the Pattersons forgave her. They were the ones with the most power over her pain. But having Wes share the burden and know her dark past and the mistakes she made, there was some hope in that, right?

Possibly not. She hadn't told him everything about Gabe because the words also opened up the door to rejection. What would he say about the horrible things she'd done?

And would she try to frame the words to cover her tracks and explain her intentions along with what transpired? But she knew that by not having told Wes already, she'd lost any benefit of the doubt.

So she told him the cold, ugly truth.

"It was drugs," she began. "We started out in ninth grade drinking beer. We didn't quite understand supply and demand—that if we drank Mr. Patterson dry, he'd find out about it. He grounded Gabe for a long, long while, and our parties at his house stopped sophomore year.

"But I wasn't done," she continued. "I didn't like the taste, but I liked the thrill of it, sneaking around. So I moved on to marijuana. I became best friends with the kid who sold it at school. My grades dropped, some friends drifted away, and I mingled with the wrong replacements. I thought I was fine. I kept my grades in the low Cs and never got arrested. During my junior year I was into the hard stuff—cocaine, other things—and my parents were on to me. They grounded me. Took away my car. Forced me into counseling. And I fought them, big-time. I threatened to move out. The day it happened, I packed a bag and jumped into a friend's car and screamed I'd never come back.

"I broke up with Gabe at the beginning of junior year. But through all of this, Gabe stayed friends with me. I can hardly believe it, looking back. I was so mean to him, but it was like he was watching out for me. He tried talking to me at school, but I wasn't having it. I'd laugh him off or act indifferent.

"That night I left my parents' house, there was a party on the other side of town. Kind of a mix between high schoolers and college kids. And all kinds of drugs. Cocaine, heroin, you name it. Word must have gotten around school the day before because Gabe called me and pleaded with me not to go.

"The party was a little messed up. That was probably one of the few times I didn't get into the drugs, not because of any willpower; I'd gotten too drunk too fast. I just drank my sorrows away. I drank and drank and eventually passed out. I woke up in the basement of the so-called friend who'd brought me to the party. She said I'd been throwing up over everything and the guy who lived there wanted me out. So she and her boyfriend dragged me into their car and then into her basement."

Emmy paused. She drew in a deep breath before continuing. "So I wasn't there. But sometime after midnight, Gabe showed up. Alone. He should have brought a few of his football buddies—he was a stranger, in high school, and it wasn't a nice crowd. People who were there said he stormed into the house screaming my name and checked every room and closet. No one told him I was gone because no one probably knew who I was—we'd gotten in based on someone else's connection.

"Eventually, he entered the master bedroom. There was a guy there, Lenny Houston, who'd gotten out of the county jail the week before. He was stoned. And he had a gun. Lenny probably thought he was a cop. So he pulled out his .45 and shot Gabe three times: once in the chest, which collapsed a lung; once in the shoulder; and once in his leg, which clipped an artery. He choked on his blood and fought for breath while his artery bled out. All of this happened while I was passed out in the basement of some girl I barely knew. He died because of me. His parents lost their youngest son . . . because of me."

Chapter 36

Wes checked his watch. The date didn't escape him: April 1, April Fool's. But there wasn't anything funny about what he was about to do.

He was half an hour early. By now, Emmy would be at the ER, immersed in broken arms and the common cold. His mother was off at some retreat in the Smoky Mountains, praying about other people's problems, including Wes's, but probably not her own. And here he sat, outside Ron's apartment, waiting to take him to jail.

He checked his e-mail for the hundredth time. In-box empty. He knew Emmy wouldn't end it that way; she'd have the courage to meet him face-to-face. He grimaced. But it was probably already over from what he had done two weeks ago, opening up her old wounds. He had wanted to be Emmy's rock and shelter, but how could he comfort her when he'd betrayed her trust? He'd failed her; he accepted it as fact even as he held her while she mourned the loss of Gabe, again, on her apartment floor. It was a reprieve, he knew, from the undeniable. The urge to use Emmy's passwords and rummage through her personal belongings had been too much. He'd realized his mistake too late.

The justifications that had bloated his mind at the time now seemed unimportant to the grand scheme of things. And the grand scheme of things was that Emmy was only weeks away from deploying and they were probably finished. And if the door was closed, it wasn't Emmy's doing. Wes had slammed it in his own face.

He stared at Ron's door. He didn't want to knock, didn't want to end his father's freedom. He thought of his mom, in no trouble with the law but trapped in a body that was slowly, methodically shutting down, pinning her in. Wes pictured his mom's head bowed, saying prayers out loud for him and Emmy, for her brothers and sisters and the mailman, maybe a token prayer for her own condition, then back to longer prayers for those around her. He imagined hands being laid on Janet's shoulders, and maybe someone bold would lay a hand in the direction of her kidneys, asking God to heal them.

But God wasn't going to heal them. Not without his mother's cooperation. They were praying for the wrong outcome. God needed to ignore the two failing kidneys and insert one life-sustaining organ through a donor. He needed a vessel . . . he *had* a vessel if his mother would take it. Who cared who it came from? Thousands of people were in front of Janet on the donor list. Why wouldn't she accept the transplant? What combination of words and timing would unlock her heart?

Ron's door opened and he came out, hands in his pockets, craning his neck to look at the sunshine beaming down, soaking in rays. Here was the man most baffling to Wes. The convict and former addict, the man who dropped his life in the sewer and then fished it out, cleaned it up, made it serviceable again. How was this guy so put together when the rest of them weren't?

The roles had changed. Completely and forever. So where did that leave him?

Ron nodded when he got in the car, but he didn't say anything, for which Wes was grateful. For months, Wes had unleashed his pent-up emotions, and Ron had weathered them. And here they were, still standing.

The two observed the world outside the Camry's windows in silence. Wes didn't start the car. Not yet.

"Why did you want to marry Mom?" he finally asked.

"Besides getting her pregnant?"

"Yes."

"I loved her. Truly. I wanted to do right by her and by you. I thought that was enough. It should have been enough."

"Emmy told me something I wasn't expecting," Wes said. "She had a friend—ex-boyfriend—who got killed in high school trying to save her from her drug use. She got heavy into using and went to this party with drugs all over the place, and her friend Gabe went looking for her. They'd broken up, but he was still trying to look out for her. She left the party early and he never found her. An ex-con at the party shot him dead."

Ron put his hand on Wes's shoulder. "That's awful," he said. "I'm sorry."

"Every year she goes back to his family to ask for forgiveness," Wes continued. "Every year they shut the door in her face. It's like neither of them want to upset the tradition so they just keep at it. You know, for a while I thought she was holding back because she was cheating on me or just not interested. I was so wrong. Emmy was crying on the floor, telling me that until the Pattersons forgive her, she'll never be able to completely move on."

"And what did you tell her?"

"I didn't say anything. I couldn't. I went through e-mails and letters and anything else I could find instead of giving her the time she needed to tell me."

Ron waited awhile before replying. "How long before she deploys?"

"Not long. A few weeks."

"Then you've got a window."

Wes turned to face Ron. He didn't have to say Wes had messed up. They both knew it. For the first time, he asked his father for advice. "How do I fix it?"

"You may not like what I'm about to say, but forgiveness ain't on terms of your own making. If there's one thing I know, it's that. Took a whole lot of years to figure it out though."

"I don't follow," Wes said. "If that's what you think, why are you here? Why have you been spending time with me?"

"I love you, you're my son, and I want to spend time with you," Ron said. "If we can make a go of this reconciling project, more's the blessings. But I haven't been showing up to try and earn your forgiveness. I sure asked you for it, back in January in Dalton. I'd been waiting for that

speech a long, long time. But I didn't ask for it with terms and conditions. I didn't ask it and then expected we'd be father and son again. We
may never be. Forgiveness ain't about making it back to where you were,
because that's time you don't get back. There's no contract for it. Can't be
earned."

"I see."

"I'd say you don't, judging by the edge in your voice," Ron said. "It's
just as much for you as for me, Wes. If you are here because you think
you're doing this out of the kindness of your heart, don't bother. I'll hop
a bus to jail. Don't matter none. If in the back of your mind, you think
you'll forgive me because of something I'll give in return, leave. The decision has to be based on you and the Almighty and whether you want to
give that to *him*. And the same goes for Emmy. It's not about her and the
Pattersons. It's about her and God and asking *him*, letting *him* in to take
care of her past. Take it and wipe it away—flesh made new, all that biblical stuff. You can give her that understanding if you'll accept it yourself.
You will always have things in your life you'll wish you could do over and
people who do you wrong or you wish would appreciate you more. Welcome to the party—I've got a marker and a name sticker for you. Doesn't
always work out, and if you're the guilty one, do you want someone to
hold it over your head? Don't work that way."

Wes thought about those words, then started the ignition.

Chapter 37

The trick with pulling yourself out of the ditch is, you can't really do it. Not on your own. Takes another hand so you can prop your feet just right, get a good angle. Takes a couple hands to give you the strength to do it.

I guess you could say that's what happened for me. I was out of jail. Vowed never to go back. Vowed a lot of things, like New Year's resolutions, and lots were broken. But there was one I'd kept—to go with Michael to a recovery ministry session. He met me at the halfway house, drove me to the meeting at a church in Roswell. I spent most of the ride wiping the sweat off my palms and onto my jeans. When we pulled up, I gave him an ultimatum, as if we were negotiating. I asked him straight up why he was doing all of this for me. He'd met me at the jail, helped me move a few boxes to the halfway house, promised to be around whenever I needed a ride. But for what? What was his angle?

"Two reasons," he told me. "I was in a tough spot as a kid, and someone helped me out. I put myself in a tough spot later in life, and again, someone gave me a chance. So there it is. I'd like to believe giving second chances is all we need."

I considered this, then agreed to go inside. Truth was, at this point I had meeting fatigue. The Alcoholics Anonymous meetings helped some, but I'd just never enjoyed public speaking, and getting in front of a room full of fellow recoveries and touching on how long I'd been without a drink or a snort made me think more about the drink or drugs and how dry my mouth felt and how much it was still ingrained in me to use the bottle to wash my worries away.

Michael walked me through the crowd. I occasionally made eye contact with the people Michael introduced, but I tried to keep my head low and suffered through the pleasantries until the meeting began.

There was a good crowd at the event—most of the rows of chairs were full. Me and Michael and one of Michael's Talking Creek friends sat close to the back and listened to what amounted to a sermon and quick prayer. Then the attendees split into small groups. Michael and Wayne, as he introduced himself, ushered me over to a specific group of four men. Michael did the handshake routine again. I wouldn't remember anyone's name that night, except Otis, and only because he was the first man I had ever seen wear an oily BP hat into church. I liked him immediately.

A full-bearded man with a Semper Fi tattoo on one forearm asked me why I'd come. I asked if this was the part where I told my sob story, and he replied I could tell whatever it was I wanted to and then we'd pray for whatever it was I wanted them to.

I started slow—where I lived, my night shift at the supermarket. I walked them through my family and how my parents were gone, my failed marriage, my boy who I hadn't seen or talked to in a long, long while. Then I delivered the jail portion, complete with arrest record and the stints I'd done so far. Whether I had the strength to stay out of jail, to not add on to the record, I didn't know, I admitted to them. I finished my testimony and all of its bitter glory and felt the

air completely sucked out of me. Each man nodded as if that
was as much their story as mine.

Otis asked what jail I'd been at, and I told him.

Strange thing happened then. "Spent a month there," Otis
said. "Pizza days were not the best."

"You should try South Georgia cuisine," another man said.
"Might as well eat cardboard. Ketchup and cardboard."

"I'll second that," said the former marine.

I asked if everyone had done time.

"Everyone except Captain America and his cohort,"
the former marine told me, pointing at Wayne and Michael.
"'Course if they hang around us much longer, who knows?"

"Well, Mike did kill a man once, but they gave him a shiny
medal for it," Otis said. "And who knows about Wayne?
Maybe one of those guys in the back of the ambulance made
him angry and he didn't give him some aspirin."

That elicited a chuckle.

"Killed a man?" I asked, turning to Michael.

"A few," he said. "And I've lost a few men under my
command too. Those hurt the most."

They all nodded grimly and transitioned to other stories.
The conversation bounced around the men in the chairs,
and I listened to each man's past. Pain, guilt, grief beyond
measure—I saw it in their eyes and their tears and heads
looking down. Their lives were filled with divorces and
estranged families and empty voice-mail machines because
their children never called.

This wasn't an experience I'd known on hallowed ground.
Church for me growing up involved singing hymns while the
pianist played an out-of-tune instrument and watching
my father stifle yawns while I drew stick figures on the
announcements during the sermons. The preacher, a man set
in his ways, with a commute that involved walking across

the street from the church-provided housing, occasionally
got into redemption and sin but never with humbled personal
experiences, always some political figure or biblical personality
that offered a transition into some random Scripture in
Romans or Acts. It made my faith detached and processed.
This was something different. We merry band of town drunks
were all under one roof, professing our grief like Job, having
lost just about as much, and turning toward each other for
encouragement. It wasn't self-help as much as fellowship. Even
Michael revealed his hurts—from battling his past to battling
the ghosts that followed him home from war. There was no
hierarchy, no judgment in the men's struggles. Only hope.

Afterward, Michael asked if I'd want to come back. I
told him I'd like that. Been going ever since, no conditions.
That's how I got pulled out.

Chapter 38

Hilton Head Shipwreck 12," Lynn read off the screen. "What's the significance there?"

Emmy shrugged. "It's an old password from high school. Hilton Head was our family vacation spot and twelve is the number of goals I scored during a soccer camp. For whatever reason that's what I stuck with. Ironclad."

Lynn jotted the password down on an index card and dropped it in a folder in her filing cabinet. "Got it."

"Thanks for taking care of this," Emmy said. "And on such short notice. It's April 9 and I don't have all my loose ends tied. My plan A didn't exactly work out, and I didn't really want my parents rummaging through passwords and bank accounts."

"It's no problem," Lynn said. "I'm a whiz at online bill pays. Once we set up our accounts for the foster-care retreat, I never went back. I don't think I've used a regular checkbook in two years." She formed a T for time-out with her hands, then rubbed Emmy's slumping shoulder. "So where did you leave things?"

Emmy looked at Lynn and tried to give her best smile. "We left them about as well as can be expected. Which is—I have no idea. I've had dates that ended on worse terms. We didn't scream at each other. There wasn't any tension like that. It was just—what was done was done; we both knew it."

"Do you miss him?"

"You have no idea," Emmy said. "I knew I'd miss him when I was deployed, but it feels too soon."

"Maybe that tells you something."

"I don't know if I can trust him again," Emmy said. "It hurts. I'd let him get closer than any guy besides one. There was a reason I never dated seriously in college or the army—because of that. I just didn't think he'd let his curiosity do that, you know?"

"You didn't think a reporter wouldn't go snooping around given a key and a question?" Lynn asked. Her eyebrow was arched in amusement.

"Yeah, okay," Emmy said, holding her hand up in mock surrender. "Kind of like putting Baxter in a back yard and not expecting him to howl at squirrels or dig at the fence line. And it's not like Wes did it to be vindictive."

"Have you tried looking at it from his perspective?" Lynn said. "I'm not taking sides," she said, responding to the look Emmy gave her. "But figuring out relationships takes some empathy."

Emmy sighed. "I've tried looking at it from his perspective—all the stuff he's found out about his parents. He was hurting, and I didn't help the situation by dodging his questions. I wasn't ready, though, to tell him. I was working my way up to it during the training cycle. I told myself that once I stopped by the Pattersons' again, then I could talk with Wes. Win or lose with them, the visit would be behind me, and who knows, maybe they'd actually talk with me and we could work something out."

"Work what out?" Lynn said. Her voice was delicate, like she was tiptoeing around glass plates.

"We'd be on speaking terms again?" Emmy offered. "I don't know. I always figured they'd come to a point where, them getting over Gabe's death, they'd allow me back in. They were practically my second family."

"Emmy, we're getting to another topic, but you have to understand, when you lose a child, or a husband, you grieve for a lifetime."

"But you're doing pretty well."

"With the support of family, and counseling sessions twice a week. I still wake up in cold sweats, still cry for no reason at all. Grief hasn't gone away."

"I didn't know."

"There was no need for you to know. Counseling isn't a weakness. It helps to cope, to recognize where your source of frustration comes from so you can tackle it instead of trying to shut it out. And sometimes I need someone else to talk to who isn't as close to it. I can't bring this on Addy. She's only eight and coming out of her grief in her own way. I don't want to saddle her with the nights I cry myself to sleep or can barely function at work because I saw a couple holding hands at the movie theater when she and I went to see a kids flick. Counseling's helped, a lot. But the point is you never get over something like that—you or them. Which means you should never, ever knock on their door again."

"I can't not try," Emmy said.

"It's in your nature to fix things, I know. You're a healer. But you're probably not helping them by reminding them each year. It's traumatic enough. Pray for them, support them from behind the scenes if there's a way to do it, even write them a letter explaining your thoughts. But after that—let them be."

Emmy nodded, then looked out the window. "How has Nate been doing at rehab?"

"He'd almost be done if he stuck to the plan. But he cracked. He went to see Mandy, and her father was adamant that he wasn't going to get through the front door. Used some pretty strong language on Nate, and it had its effect. Nate's parents weren't happy he went there unannounced either, so he's skipped the last couple of sessions. I found out all of this from his mother, mind you. He did answer his phone once when I called—said he was at his grandparents' boathouse on Lake Allatoona and wouldn't budge until he got to speak with Mandy."

"That's childish," Emmy said.

"He can't see it, at least not yet," Lynn said. "I just hope his grandparents are keeping a close eye on him. You do strange things when you're hurt, especially at that age."

Chapter 39

Walking with Paul through Tributary's campus on a bright, humid, mid-April day, Wes thought that the pair must have been a sight for the undergrads—Wes in his shorts and ball cap, Paul the tenured professor in his regular campus attire with sport coat and slacks.

Wes had requested this meeting with Paul. The deadline for his paper was approaching, and he was out of ideas. Actually, he had plenty of ideas, a half dozen written and sent to Paul throughout the semester, but each had been rejected.

Wes's grades on the other class assignments weren't the problem. He nailed the pop quizzes and tests. It was the absence of the biggest grade of the year that bothered him. Like a source left unchecked, and all the more frustrating because he had continually pursued it. He wasn't avoiding it. More like Paul was avoiding Wes's work, trying to lead him on to something else. And the more Wes thought about it, the more he wanted the air cleared between the two.

They arrived on the main campus stretch—two brick roads, trademarks of Tributary, and a large green lawn running down the middle. Interspersed in the field were tall oaks and a handful of benches. Wes found an empty bench where they could begin their meeting.

"I'm glad you don't mind us getting a breath of fresh air," Paul said. "The office can get stuffy, more so during the winter months, but I find myself using any and every excuse to go outside and take in the sights and smells of the campus."

"Works for me," Wes said. "Before I get into the school matters, I wanted to say thanks to you and Betty for sending my mom the flowers and the letter. That was very kind."

"She's in our prayers every day, as are you," Paul said with a warm smile.

Wes considered the professor. He wore the two hats of a compassionate man and firm instructor quite well, despite their recent differences. It was one of the reasons Wes had enrolled at Tributary. The Pauls of the world were at a premium. Short supply and running out. Wes had known it and seized the opportunity.

Except, he hadn't anticipated Paul carrying the instruction over to Wes's personal life. He understood the rules could be stretched at a university like Tributary and that there was some benefit to it. But in this one specific subject, a paper about a Civil War soldier's letters, Paul was on a nonacademic mission.

"So here it is," Wes said. "I know about you telling Ron about my mom's condition. I know that's why he traveled up to Tennessee to see the doctor. I bet you two talked, and he's not mad at you because you never told him to go and try anything like that. A few months ago, I probably would have been furious. But now I'm just tired."

Paul was silent.

"I appreciate what you've done for me," Wes said. "I absolutely love your class and the way you teach. But this isn't the same. You want me to repeat the work I did two years ago as Michael's last request. Paul, with all due respect, I'm not giving your son's eulogy here."

"I would defend my intentions by saying that the objective of the class is a multifaceted education richer than any other university can provide," Paul said. "It's unique, but I firmly believe the assignment is paramount to the education and intent of the course."

"I've done everything you've asked this semester in grading papers and putting the extra work in. I'm putting my own money into this degree, an education—not an intervention. The first time we met, you challenged me on some principles, you got me to thinking about the lines I could cross and the price to pay," Wes said. "I realize that sometimes in searching for knowledge, we may look in the wrong places for things that we want to see. Have you applied that philosophy here? Are you trying to finish something your son started?"

Paul looked at him hard. For the first time since he'd known Paul, Wes didn't back down and look away. But Paul made an unexpected move, extending his hand with his palm open. "Do you have any reading materials? A Bible, perhaps."

Wes grunted, but opened his backpack and retrieved his Bible. Paul thumbed to the Gospels and then to Luke and showed Wes a verse.

"The Prodigal Son," Wes said. "I had a feeling you were going there."

Paul nodded. "From what I have seen of Benjamin Watkins's letters, there is a familiar theme."

"Explains how quick you were to suggest I bring Ron on the Civil War trips. But I don't see a connection."

"Are you sure?" Paul asked. "Benjamin had a homecoming, did he not? He survived the war, but during it he often lamented in what state he would return. He was a small piece of a larger movement, and it affected him deeply."

Paul closed the Bible and looked at the clouds. "But you've given me something to consider, Wes," he said. "Now that my opinion on the topic is known, you're allowed to write in whatever direction you see fit. You're short on time, but I've seen you work on tighter deadlines and come through splendidly. So I'll push you there. Fair?"

"A better proposition than I had five minutes ago."

Wes extended his hand, and Paul shook it.

Chapter 40

Wes stood still, alternately looking over the quiet hills of Allatoona Pass and the two old photos in his hand.

One photo he printed out from the historical site showed the pass itself, an old railroad cut that for a few hours in 1864 was a bloody Civil War battlefield where Benjamin Watkins's division fought. Any steps Wes took could easily have traced his ancestor's.

He centered the historic photo on the hood of his car and gazed out at the massive railroad cut in front of him. In the old photo, two dirt hills topped with star forts stood on either side of the cut. In between the hills lay the Western and Atlantic Railroad line. Buildings surrounded the railroad tracks once it left the cut, but trees were scarce.

He looked at the cut now. A hiking trail ran through the railroad's old bed. The railroad had been moved. The tiny town of Allatoona that should have been behind him was now underwater. To Wes's right was Lake Allatoona, and he could hear a handful of Jet Skis getting an early start to the day. The terrain surrounding the railroad cut was now forest, with pine trees two stories high guarding the old forts. Ghosts were rumored to visit the battlefield, now a park.

Wes turned his attention to the second photo, taken from his mom's photo album the last time he visited. In front of the railroad cut, Ron held a tiny Wes high in his arms, both father and son smiling. Janet wore hiker's shorts and a tank top and looked the picture of health. On that day, they would have hiked the cut and picnicked outside of it, tickled, and chased their young son, do all the things young families do.

History. American and Watkins. Paul Gavin didn't have Allatoona Pass on his syllabus because the battle happened after the fall of Atlanta. But for Wes, his research for his term paper ended here, and so, too did his family's. Their trip to Allatoona as a happy family happened before their upheaval, and it made the most sense for him to piece together the revelations of the last few months by starting here.

There was only one other car in the parking lot, at the far end and parked crooked, taking up a handful of spaces. More people were probably interested in water sports and cruising the lake than hiking in this humid weather. Wes was hoping for the solitude.

He looked up at the sky. "I guess we should go for a walk, huh?"

On the well-worn path, he listened to his footsteps. He approached the first historical marker and readjusted his backpack and looked again toward the parking lot. He sat on the trail and pulled out a copy of one of Benjamin's letters and read it aloud.

> We are at the spur of the ridge and being swept back toward the Redoubt.

Wes looked at the rise in the terrain on his left, which would have been where Benjamin's regiment came into the battle. But the area, which had been cleared, was now saturated with tall pine trees. It was hard to imagine the area as anything more than nature's playground.

> We advanced on a line of works which had been abandoned. Oh, my heart soared for a brief instant, but I should have known better. Did we crush the Yankees at Cass, or Dalton, or at Kennesaw? No, they just kept coming as we stumbled over ourselves. Here, perhaps we had an advantage, but it was soon negated, as their forces across the cut and behind breastworks put forth a withering fire. I could hear the metal slapping the bodies of men around me. I expected much the same fate but continued onward.

Wes stopped reading and walked into the middle of the railroad cut. The sunshine dimmed and the temperature cooled inside the cut—both sides were nearly two stories high and filled with trees and brush. Wes thought the ghost hunters probably attributed the temperature drop to the presence of spirits, and he laughed. There were ghosts in the cut all right, but familiar ones, and he wasn't running from them.

Maybe Benjamin's ghost was up there near the earthworks. It wasn't until the Mississippi regiment's colonel signaled for the retreat that a mini ball slammed into Benjamin's foot, crushing bones before it exited. Benjamin had hobbled back down, forever maimed.

"The story of my family," Wes said aloud. He looked to the sky, for what he didn't know. A response? Was he supposed to expect a response to prayer? He kept talking because he felt he had an audience.

"Are we all wounded, is that it? Ron is a mess, but a well-meaning mess. Mom's got a way to get better, but she won't take it. They both made or almost made incredibly impactful decisions as parents. And somehow, the woman I love, whom I let down, she's pieced herself together after a horrible accident in high school. It was an accident, right? Am I looking at it correctly? She didn't pull the trigger. She wasn't even at the party. But she blames herself, and the Pattersons blame her, and Gabe isn't talking because he's not here anymore."

He paused. "How do I help them?" he whispered. He looked up again, letting the light piercing the forest warm his face. "How do I fix me?" he said, softer.

He lowered his gaze again to the far reaches of the railroad cut. Then he squinted, even with the shade, thinking his vision was hazy. He couldn't be seeing what he was seeing.

But he knew God had answered him, had put a response in his path, and he couldn't neglect it or turn away. He walked, then jogged, then ran to the far end of the cut.

Off to the side in a bed of overgrown weeds was a young man, curled in a ball, face pale and body cold, dying.

Chapter 41

Emmy pecked away at the keyboard for the nurses' station computer, entering notes from her ER rounds, when she heard the whoosh of the ER entrance, even behind the closed double doors that separated the waiting room from the treatment area. She didn't look up—someone else was triaging and she didn't hear directions coming from a paramedic bringing in an urgent case. But a few minutes later, Sue appeared over the nurses' station. "You ought to see this," she said. Emmy followed her to the second room, where Nate Stroud lay, an IV already tapped.

"Pneumonia," Sue said. "His fever was 103 when we first took it. He collapsed overnight in a park a mile away from the marina where his grandparents' houseboat is docked."

Emmy focused on the care he needed. They would drain his lungs and he'd spend the night in the ICU, getting pumped full of antibiotics.

"He'd be in a lot worse shape if Wes hadn't brought him in."

A gasp escaped from Emmy's lips. "Please tell me he hasn't already left."

Sue pointed toward the waiting room. Emmy rushed through the double doors. Wes sat in one corner, staring absently at the TV. He was almost as pale as Nate. There were dirt stains on his knees and sweat stains on his shirt. His eyes were bloodshot and there were smudges of dirt on his face. He'd probably stumbled getting Nate into his car. Wes saw her approaching but didn't move.

"When is the last time you've eaten?" Emmy said.

"That kid was stubborn, even half dead. He would only come here,"

Wes said weakly, ignoring her question. "He wouldn't let me take him to a closer hospital. I'm sorry."

"You're blood sugar has got to be low," she said. She rushed back behind the double doors and reappeared with some orange juice and cookies. Wes nodded and began to eat and drink. They sat in silence as he finished.

"I went there to pray," he said. "To think . . . be with God. First time I've done that in . . . I don't know how long. And I stumble on a kid who is basically trying to off himself. How's that for an answer to prayer?"

Emmy wiped some of the dirt from Wes's face.

"It *was* an answered prayer, for him," she said. "And his parents. And probably Mandy. Me too."

"He kept muttering about Mandy," Wes said, "saying he'd rather not live without her and wasn't going to try."

"I will call his parents," Emmy said. "I have half a mind to call Mandy's too and stop this nonsense, but I don't think her father will listen. He thinks he's trying to protect her by separating them."

"And he'll end up hurting her too, probably worse," Wes said. He rubbed his eyes, exhaustion setting in. "You were right. We always end up hurting the ones we love worse than anyone else can."

Emmy looked away.

"How do you help them?" Wes said. "What possible chance do we have against ourselves? It's just a cycle that won't ever stop. My mom and dad. Nate and Mandy. You and Gabe. Me and you . . ."

Wes stopped. He forced himself to stand. Emmy put her hand on his chest to stop him.

"Not before we check your blood sugar," Emmy said. He pulled out his Accu-Chek, stuck a finger on his left hand and checked the results.

"You're borderline," she said.

"I'm fine," Wes said.

"Please stay," Emmy said.

"Are you kidding? With my deductible?" Wes said in an attempt at humor.

"You know what I mean," Emmy said.

For a moment, their eyes stayed on each other, with so much to say but no words coming.

"I was working on something at Allatoona. I'm real close. Have to finish." He rushed out before Emmy could say anything more.

Chapter 42

The dialysis lines flowed from machine to body. There were about a dozen of these machines in the clinic, some in a large room and a few in isolated rooms for people with communicable diseases. The machines in the large room were lined up along a wall like soldiers in formation, with a reclining chair beside each one and two foldout tables on either side of the reclining chair. Patients sat in the recliners while nurses and technicians floated from station to station. Wes spotted his mom in the middle of the room.

He'd spent the two nights after the Allatoona incident working on his term paper. He'd finished the first draft just in time to drive up for his mom's first treatment. He desperately needed time to process, but he needed to see his mother more.

"So this is dialysis," Wes said. The description and low-res pictures online didn't do it justice. It looked more like a scene out of *Star Wars* or *Star Trek*, humans hooked up to machines to become cyborgs or to get fingers, arms, or legs replaced by robotic ones. Except these patients weren't warriors as much as survivors, most of them with other chronic ailments.

The smell of antiseptic hung in the air as one of the nearby chairs was wiped down and thoroughly disinfected by a nurse. Wes cringed at the smells and sights of a clinic, needles, and treatments. It was easier for him to accept his body's failings than this, seeing so many people like his mother dependent on technology for functions their organs would no longer perform.

Janet was watching TV when he arrived. She turned to look at Wes, her face strained.

"You're late," she whispered.

"Got tied up in traffic in Chattanooga," he said. "But I called your sister and told her I'll stay with you and be able to drive you home." Wes sat in a chair beside her and the machines. A large catheter was stuck into her arm as if her body were a car engine getting ready to be flushed. Wes shuddered. "Does it hurt?"

"It's uncomfortable, but not painful, no."

"How often will you have to do this?"

"Twice a week."

Wes nodded. "School's out pretty soon. I'll just take one class in the summer, so I can be up here for a lot of these. With Emmy deploying and us pretty much over, I guess you and I will be seeing plenty of each other, if you can stand it."

"Of course I can stand it." A tear welled in her eye.

Wes looked away. "When does Dr. Benewitz come in to check on you?" he asked.

"Once a month, probably. But the nurses and technicians here are taking good care of me. I'll just have to get used to daytime TV instead of fielding purchasing orders at the office."

Wes nodded again. He opened his computer bag. "A few things to keep you occupied so you don't become too familiar with the daytime soaps." He pulled out a portable DVD player, three romantic comedies, two paperback books, and magazines. "Take your pick," he said. He put them on the table beside her one by one.

The last item he pulled out was a scrapbook. He put it in her lap.

"My own son, scrapbooking? Now who put you up to that? Who *paid* you?"

Wes shrugged. "I've been sifting through our old family photos from the box I kept. Decided to put a scrapbook together of the photos that didn't make the original cut in the albums. I felt bad for them—kind of like the kid who gets picked last for kickball. I used a few new ones too.

The old ones are from the box I have at my house. Ironically it helped me finish the paper."

Mom's eyes held a distant gaze at the mention of the storage shed, as if the discovery now tainted what she held in her hands. Then she drew in a deep breath, as if preparing for a confrontation with her son

"I didn't come to talk about that," Wes said in a soft voice. "Or ever. That's not why I'm here. And I didn't come to try and convince you of your treatment options. You are a grown woman and can make decisions without your son being snippety about it. Just know that anything I suggested or want for you, ultimately it's because you're my mom and I love you and I hate to see you in pain. I plan on being here for as many of these treatments as I can, for as long as you are on them. Okay?"

"Okay." She patted his hand.

Wes wondered if history was destined to repeat itself. Had his mom and grandmother had similar conversations over a dialysis unit? What would his grandmother have done if she'd been offered a kidney under similar circumstances? Would she take the gift from the person who'd hurt her the most? Had Wes's grandmother known anyone like that?

Wes closed his eyes and said a brief prayer, hoping those invisible words could float through the air, sift into the tubes attached to his mother, filter into her body, and help ease her past pains so she could be free of this disease and these machines, forever.

But his prayer, he realized, did more for him, helping him keep himself removed from the choices he couldn't make and the people he couldn't control. He opened his eyes and smiled. "Seeing as we have the time, I am going to allow you a courtesy that no self-respecting twentysomething male has done before. I'm going to sit here and let you tell me about how cute or crazy a kid I was. And I'll let you do it the rest of the treatment. How much longer is it?"

"One hour," a nurse said, who'd overheard their conversation. She pulled up a chair. "And honey, it's not just your momma who's going to listen in."

Wes glanced around the room. Another nurse and technician were looking over his mother's shoulder at the scrapbook and the baby picture on the first page. He groaned. "Oh boy. Think I made a tactical mistake."

"It wouldn't be the first time," Janet said, pointing to a picture and holding it up for the audience to see. "Remember when you fell out of the tree house across the street from our apartment and knocked out a tooth?"

Chapter 43

When Wes blinked, dots of red ink filled his thoughts, tracing sentences and paragraphs and thoughts he'd written, edited, and rewritten. He concentrated hard on the steps he took up the stairs of Tributary's liberal arts building, fighting exhaustion and little sleep. Physically, he was spent by the Allatoona episode on Saturday, the hours after the hospital to write most of the paper, then his visit to Nashville on Monday. Mentally, he'd used up that tank on the paper he turned in Tuesday. So when he arrived at Professor Gavin's office, he was already on his heels, bracing himself for what promised to be a lengthy discussion of the utter failure of a semester paper he'd turned in, or at least he thought. A paper graded within twenty-four hours couldn't be a good sign.

He was completely unprepared for what met him when he knocked and opened the professor's door. Or rather, who.

"Hey Wes," said Lewis Banner, *North Georgia News* sports and city editor, his former boss. He had a reporter's notebook in hand and a digital recorder on Paul's desk. The two looked like they'd been having a cordial conversation before Wes walked in.

Paul saw the confused look on Wes's face and headed it off. "Mr. Banner called me a half hour ago regarding an assignment."

Wes turned to Lewis. "Assignment?"

"Starks," Lewis said, shaking his head. "Word has gotten around about your daring rescue."

Keith Starks, the *News*'s managing editor, Lewis's boss. Wes had butted heads with him, and ultimately resigned. He'd been the one to assign Michael's obituary to Wes and had hovered over him like a helicopter parent, trying to sway how the story progressed and what Wes would say.

The rift hadn't been enough to keep Wes's byline out of the paper. Lewis had fed him freelance work, which wouldn't have happened without Starks's approval. Now this. Wes took the seat next to Lewis with a heavy sigh. "There was nothing daring about it."

"But there were two newsworthy aspects," Lewis said. "One: a high school star lay barely conscious in a park. Two: he was rescued by a *North Georgia News* contributor."

"And Starks figured you'd be the best person to get the story out of me," Wes said. He glanced at Paul, who was practically reclining in his seat, hands propped behind his head, smiling.

Paul saw his glance. "I'm amused at the irony, Wes. You've spent a great deal of time chronicling heroic feats. How does it feel to be among such nobility?"

"You're kidding, right?" Wes said. "I'm no hero."

Paul set his hands down in his lap as if to give a lecture. "No? Then by what definition would a hero be heroic?"

"Guys like Michael, like you," Wes said. "Or Benjamin Watkins."

Lewis, who had been scribbling notes, looked to Paul for confirmation.

"Wes's ancestor," Paul said. "Fought at the Battle of Allatoona Pass."

"And I haven't said any of this is on the record," Wes said, making eye contact with Lewis.

"Come on, Wes," Lewis said. "You've got to give me something. This is a pretty significant story for Talking Creek."

"This could end horribly for the kid," Wes said. "Paul, you were there when your son made a mistake. What would have happened if it made the newspapers? Nate needs some time to heal."

"Well, his family isn't talking," Lewis said. "And I suppose you aren't either, considering this is off the record. What can you give me that's on the record?"

Wes groaned. "I was walking the battlefield, trying to piece together my research paper when I found him at the end of the railroad cut. I rushed him to the hospital, went home, took a nap, started writing a paper that my professor probably destroyed with a red pen, and here I am."

"What Wes has neglected to tell you, Mr. Banner, is that more than 150 years ago, Benjamin Watkins dragged a wounded man from his company away from that battlefield, before he was wounded himself. That wounded man ended up becoming an elected official of the great state of Arkansas. The governor, in fact."

Lewis had a sparkle in his eye as he jotted the information down. "Wes," he said, emphatically. "You have *got* to give me something. This is great stuff."

"How about his research paper?" Paul said. "That is, if Wes is willing to release it."

"You're joking," Wes said.

"I was about to discuss it with Wes, you see," Paul said, not taking his eyes off Lewis. "Rough around the edges, but the meat of it is fantastic. How does a soldier, during war, deal with what he can and cannot control? How does a man in a sixty-thousand-man army square his fate that, in so many aspects, is not under his control? He can no more influence the generals than he can the bullets flying around him. In such an environment where chaos abounds, it is hard to keep one's head. You begin to think, 'Why did I survive the battle when better men around me fell? How can I return to my family in the condition I'm in? How fleeting is the glory and how deeply saddening is the loss?' And yet, through one of the most bloody battles in the Civil War, Benjamin Watkins discovered a small measure of himself, something he could in fact control. In war you cannot stand still and lament your mistakes or those of your army. You must press on, for choosing to stand still is to surely die. It's a riveting paper, Mr. Banner."

Wes sat, mouth open. Paul grinned and slid the paper to Lewis, who looked at Wes for confirmation. Wes closed his mouth and nodded.

Lewis clicked the digital recorder off and stood up.

"Starks is going to edit this so it's about the *North Georgia News* and its outreach, isn't he?" Wes said.

Lewis chuckled. "I'll see what I can salvage. Maybe all of it, but you know he'll get an opinion column in there about all the good things former and current staff do for Talking Creek. Unless you want this to be about Nate."

"Not yet," Wes said.

"Yet?"

"Give me a week. Then I might have a story for you."

Lewis nodded and closed the door behind him.

"So," Paul said. He still had the look of a man thoroughly enjoying himself. "About your grade."

Chapter 44

A dish on Janet's coffee table overflowed with cookies and an assortment of pastries. Betty Gavin took a bite of one of the cookies and gave Janet an approving nod, but Paul wasn't hungry. He adjusted the collar of his button-up shirt. *Nervous*, he confessed to himself.

He cleared his throat as if about to give a lengthy lecture. "Janet, thank you for humoring us and allowing us to visit," he began. "Humoring me, mainly."

"Well, you're the ones who drove all this way," Janet said. "You've done so much for Wes, and for me. It's hard to believe this is the first time we've met. Your letters have been very encouraging as I've been going through dialysis." She smiled. "Besides, it's been such a long time since I'd had a parent-teacher conference."

"If only I *could* have those," Paul said. "Would do some of my undergraduate students a world of good, I'm sure. Has Wes told you anything about his history class with me?"

"Just that you were giving him a hard time with the semester paper," Janet said. "And that you'd wanted him to include the old letters he got from his father."

"Indeed, and he worked them into his essay quite well," Paul said. "If I can indulge for a minute, I believe my insistence led to some better writing from him and other unintended good fortunes."

Betty jabbed him in the ribs. "But that's not why we're here," she said. "Paul owes you an apology."

"Of sorts," Paul said. Betty's eyes bored into her husband, who flinched. "Of sorts, my lovely wife. Let me explain myself if I may."

Janet sat more defensively in her chair. Paul reached into his briefcase and pulled out a copy of the *North Georgia News* and handed it to her. "If you would, read the first three paragraphs," he said.

He watched as Janet's eyes worked their way from Lewis Banner's byline to the lead, and then to the description of what Wes had done. She turned to where the story jumped inside, a look of incredulity on her face. "This happened just a few days ago?"

Paul nodded. "On a research trip for his paper, of sorts."

"And he didn't tell me," Janet said, her eyes now distant.

"Paul, you need to get to your apology instead of just upsetting Wes's mom," Betty said.

"I'm fine," Janet said. "There's been a lot of secrets uncovered, I guess. Wes found out a big one about—" She looked up, thinking she'd said too much, then waved herself off. "I'm guessing that your being here is evidence you know about the adoption."

"He told me about the papers, but I haven't pressed him for more," Paul said. "I've pressed enough, frankly. It's a trait either I passed on to my son, Michael, or he passed on to me."

Paul spent the next few minutes trying to explain himself. How he'd prayed before turning in his retirement papers and in walked Wes, and along with him an opportunity to finish something worthwhile, to try and guide this young man from visualizing grace to experiencing forgiveness. How he'd plotted behind the scenes to get Wes and Ron together on the Civil War trails, to get them talking and maybe with a little bit of God's grace to work up a dialogue that could lead to some healing. He hadn't anticipated Janet's kidney transplant, or the adoption papers that could have sent Wes into state care, or Ron's reckless pursuit to make amends for his sins by giving Janet a new life. Paul took responsibility for his role, he told Janet, and he felt terrible he'd created such a mess out of something he had nothing but the best intentions for.

"God opens the door," he said, "but he doesn't always give us the step-by-step instructions. And there are times when he just wants us to observe and pray. I was intrusive when I should have been supportive. So you have my apologies."

Janet looked down at her clenched hands and purposefully relaxed them. "When I was seven, in the back seat of my mom's station wagon, playing with a Barbie, a light pierced the window shield and hit me between the eyes." She looked up and continued. "The next moment, I was screaming. A wave of nausea rolled through me. It concerned my mother enough to pull off to the side of the road. But once I collected my breath, the nausea lifted. When we crested the hill coming into town, we saw a head-on collision that had just happened. I looked at my mom's pale face and white knuckles and knew that an angel had brushed our lives to save us.

"When I was twenty-one, another light came through storm clouds and a hospital window. It pierced the curtain in the one open spot and distracted me from the wails of the newborn child I wanted to give over to the state. Ron was waving his arms and saying something in a desperate attempt to make me want to keep the child. But the paperwork and state case worker outside the room provided what I thought was my only option. Then the light.

"I shielded my eyes and remembered that car ride, and my heart skipped. I drew my baby boy closer to my chest and sucked in fresh air. It felt like my lungs hadn't breathed so lightly in years. Wes hushed as if he was comforted by the same air. He gazed at me with eyes completely inexperienced and needy. So I looked at the light, felt its warmth on my forehead, and knew God was talking to me again, asking me to pull off to the side of the road and consider. So I did. Sometimes he messes up our plans on purpose, Professor Gavin."

There was silence in the room. Then Janet spoke again. "What I want to know is, how did you do it? The man who caused the wreck that killed your unborn baby—how could you adopt his son?"

She was talking about Michael's past, and the mention of it put a lump in Paul's throat. The question was one of the reasons they'd kept it quiet—for one, they didn't want any kind of empathy or notoriety. They wanted to raise the child God had given them to the best of their ability and without any well-meaning but still distracting narratives about their son and his story. Michael had essentially given them permission to open up about his adoption with Wes's discovery and eulogy.

It was still a subject Paul wasn't used to discussing. But he looked at Janet and knew by her pained expression that she wasn't asking out of curiosity. It was desperation, to find solace in her own life and its tragedies.

But Paul couldn't find the words to give her.

Then Betty leaned forward and took Janet's hands into hers. "Why do you think we did it?" she asked with a gentle voice. Janet had no words but looked as if she was pleading for Betty to tell her.

Betty reached into her purse and pulled out a plastic sandwich bag. Inside was a yellow, faded newspaper clipping. "It's his obituary from the *Columbus Ledger*," she said. "Michael's biological father. They had done a few articles on the accident, and Paul collected them. A few weeks after the accident, I found the pile of them in his study. I threw them in the trash, but at the top was this one article—the obituary of the man who'd made me miscarry. I grabbed it with every intent of ripping it into tiny pieces, but something made me look.

"My body hurt, and I knew the only thing I'd be carrying for a long time was sadness and hatred, but when I saw Michael's name, I couldn't do it anymore. That wreck had ruined enough lives. I couldn't sit there and let it ruin a child's. We adopted Michael because he needed a home, and we needed to heal, and forgiving his father was the only way to move on. Otherwise we'd be stuck at the scene of the accident the rest of our lives, and he would too."

Chapter 45

The color matched. Make. Model. License plate too. Only the driver didn't fit. Someone besides Ron Watkins was driving Ron Watkins's truck.

Wes had pulled into Ron's apartment complex to check in on the place and the F-250. Ron had paid his rent ahead and shut off the utilities until he got out. He'd asked if Wes could have a look around periodically and drive his rig a few times so the gas didn't settle and tires deflate. Today, Wes's plan had been to drive the F-250 to a nearby baseball game, make fifty dollars for a feature on one of Talking Creek's starting pitchers, and then return the rig. Someone else, though, beat him to it.

Wes followed the truck for a mile. The driver put on his left blinker, and Wes pulled behind him in the left-turn lane, then into a shopping center. *Good,* Wes thought, *he's out in the open.* Through his sunglasses, Wes stared into the F-250's front mirror—and saw a large, white BP hat on the driver.

Otis.

He watched Otis hop out of the truck and run into the store. He almost called 911, but he remembered all the times his father had "dropped off the truck at the repair place." That almost brand-new truck that he took care of like an overprotective parent. Wes parked three rows over and walked over to the truck, peered into the truck bed and passenger cabin. Nothing. Immaculate. He went back to his car and grabbed a hat before he headed to the back of the store and started his search. He poked his head down each aisle and finally spotted Otis in the lumber section, wheeling a cart down the aisle with what looked like a full load of two-by-fours.

Wes hung by the tools section as Otis paid for the lumber and wheeled the cart out. Then he trailed a few paces behind as Otis exited the store. He was in luck—Otis left the lumber by the contractors' exit to bring the F-250 around.

Otis spotted Wes standing beside the lumber when he drove up in the truck. His expression went from puzzled to pale, and he slowly turned off the engine, then hopped out to face Wes. "Hi there, Wes. Look, this ain't what you think."

Wes looked for a gun but didn't see one. He knew the man's rap sheet, had read it online after they first met. Money laundering. Stolen cars. He and a business partner were caught, charged, thrown in jail. Ron had told Wes that Otis, like him, was a reformed man. But he'd just taken a truck and was about to load it with lumber to do who knew what with. Maybe he had Ron's credit card.

Wes was ready to call the cops, but he kept his phone in his pocket. It wasn't all that long ago that Wes had marched through Emmy's closet and her past, looking for answers that weren't worth what he forfeited in the process. It was a new feeling, shame, but he wore it well enough to empathize with the former convict standing in front of him.

"It may not be what I think it is," he said. "So tell me. What is it?"

Otis took off his hat and scratched his head. "Better if I show you." He flipped his hat back on. "Help me with these boards?"

★　★　★

Wes agreed to ride in the F-250 instead of following. He didn't know why. He realized, pulling out of the shopping center, that he was leaning on the passenger-side door, arms out in the defensive, like Otis was going to make a play for the glove compartment and pull out a gun. *Stop it,* he thought. *Just stop going through these ideas.*

Otis didn't seem to notice. "Only a few miles from here," he said.

"Did you drive the truck yesterday?"

Otis frowned. "How'd you guess?"

"New coat of wax," Wes said.

"Well, I suppose Ron would want his truck looking and running good. The least I could do for him."

"He's let you drive this before."

"Lots of times."

"What did you need with a big truck?" Wes said.

"You mean, 'What is the convict up to with a truck that ain't his?'"

"That's not what I meant."

"It's what you wanted to ask," Otis said. "And that's fine with me. You go to jail; you get these questions. But you'll see for yourself."

Otis pulled the truck into a large church parking lot. At the far end was a skeleton of a house, waiting for more wood, drywall, and paint to complete it. As they drove near, Wes could see men putting shingles on the roof. The sound of buzz saws and hammers drowned out the street noise.

"A Habitat house," Wes said. Otis nodded and parked the truck a few spots away from the construction.

A tall man with a thick beard and swollen arms waved toward the truck and trotted over. Wes noticed a large marine tattoo running down his arm.

"That's Jimmy," said Otis. "Or Lance Corporal, whatever you want to call him."

"Should I call him Lance Corporal so he doesn't get mad?"

Otis smiled. "Jimmy don't get mad at much anymore, 'cept when the Braves lose."

Wes hopped out of the truck with Otis. Jimmy's smile morphed into a questioning look when he saw Wes.

"Got the lumber like you asked, plus one of Ron's kin," Otis said. He handed the keys to Wes. "You can check with Ron, but he wanted us to put any extra runs for supplies on his card. The charity will eventually reimburse him, but knowing Ron, he'll tithe it right back."

"Ron's son," Jimmy said, acknowledging the connection. "Pleasure to meet you, young man."

Wes nodded and shook the man's massive, outstretched hand.

"Ron's boy thought I was stealing his truck," Otis said, patting him on the shoulder. "It's okay. I would have thought the same thing. And fifteen years ago I'd probably be doing what you thought I was doing. Glad you could see what your father and his buddies have been up to."

"Actually, Otis, I thought you might be hauling freight the feds or cops wanted," Wes said. "That was one theory anyway."

"Do what?" Otis said.

"Ron's out-of-state accident—he wouldn't tell me specifics. I had to find out from my mom's doctor. And he was always 'taking the truck into the shop.' Didn't add up."

"You've got a very active imagination," Jimmy said.

"It's gotten me in a lot of trouble lately," Wes admitted. "Too much trouble. That's why I just went ahead and rode with Otis instead of calling the cops."

"You were going to call the cops? Imagine that. Arrested at a home improvement store for buying supplies for a Habitat for Humanity house. That would have made quite a day."

"Well, it didn't happen, did it?"

"So what was your other theory?" Jimmy asked.

"Car hunting," Wes said. He put his hands in his pockets. "I thought Otis and my dad were searching for his old Corvette."

Otis burst out laughing. "Not even close," Otis said. "On the make." He grabbed a nearby hammer and handed it to Wes. "Best cure for an active mind is an active body. So what do you say, son? Help us with this house, and we'll tell you a few things about your father you may not have known. Like how he and I have been hunting for his papa's old beat-up Ford pickup truck and what he left inside it."

Chapter 46

In a corner of the room, a little boy played with a stack of blocks. From the looks of it, he was building a castle, adding to his creation, piece by piece, oblivious to his surroundings. Oblivious to the other boys and girls running around the room, or the parents talking in hushed tones, some of them wearing the bright orange garb of inmates at the county jail.

That could have been me, Wes thought. Except Ron's excommunication had been more severe, the thread snapped instead of strained. Wes at that age wouldn't have cared that his dad was in jail, wouldn't have noticed the looks in school or the burden worn by his mother. He wouldn't have noticed the pain in his father's eyes either—only the castle, his own little world of color-clashing plastic pieces that he built with his own small hands.

Wes watched the father watching his son. What did it matter, anyway, what the rest of the world thought outside these walls? Wasn't this man paying his debt? When he was released for shoplifting or drug abuse or whatever he was in for, would his neighbors and friends still be there to lend a hand, to help him recover a sliver of what was left and rebuild provisions for his family? He studied the mom, her eyes pointing toward her son, but vacant. He saw the strain in her body, her defeated shoulders. He wondered if this couple would make it or get a divorce, which parent the castle-building little boy would side with, how their lives would play out when the father's sentence ended.

The door buzzed, and Ron entered the visitation area in a bright orange uniform. Wes rose and gave him a firm handshake, and the two sat down.

"Met some friends of yours the other day," Wes said. "Otis, Jimmy, and a couple more." He held up his hands. "And I've got a ton of calluses to show for it."

"The Habitat house!" Ron said.

"It's almost a house," Wes said. "But I hope they get an inspector in there because my carpentry skills are pretty awful."

"Seems like you didn't inherit my carpentry and repair skills like I didn't inherit my father's white-collar ways," Ron said with a smile.

"Why didn't you tell me that's what you were doing this whole time?" Wes asked.

"Why'd you need to know?"

"It would have set my mind at ease," Wes said. "For a while I thought you and Otis were breaking the law."

"We were—years ago and in different circles. Jimmy too. We changed, just have that past in common. What else did they tell you?"

Wes shrugged. "A few funny stories, here and there. That you and these guys have been building these houses for a while. Doing good. And I believe them."

Ron leaned back. "Surprised you would say that. You're more of the skeptical kind."

"Not so much these days. Heard a whopper of a story that could be true that I wouldn't have believed awhile ago—that you and Otis have been searching for an old Ford pickup truck sold to a used-car dealer in Dallas, Georgia, two decades ago. With something inside the dashboard you think is still there."

"That *is* a whopper of a tale," Ron said. "You believe it?"

Wes nodded. "Thought it was the Corvette."

"Safe assumption—Vette's more flashy. But I'm going to find that truck," Ron said. "Just a matter of time."

"When you get out of here," Wes said, "I'll help you find it."

"And what makes you think you'd have more luck?"

Wes grinned. "Hello? Reporter? I get to looking for things—I eventually find them. Or they find me, it seems. I'm the finder, and you're the fixer."

Chapter 47

The last time I saw Michael Gavin was the first time I heard about his plan to have you deliver his eulogy. I realize this is a slight divergence of what I'd written you earlier, saying I didn't know what he was doing. Technically, he didn't tell me. But I figured it out, and by this point, his cancer was set in and his mind was made up. I didn't think it'd work, and for the longest time I was right. Then a little while after he passed, you called, and here I am back with the pen trying to explain myself.

I'm sure you want to know more about him. Last time I saw him, you can probably picture it. He sat on the back-porch swing, looking out over the pond. Paul was with him, of course. Although autumn was within shouting distance, the temperature was still warm, but Michael was wrapped in a blanket and wore a red Georgia hat with a picture of a growling bulldog in the center.

I told him he looked awful. He laughed. Told me most folks said he's looking great, so he appreciated the sincerity. Said his cancer was going to win—they all knew it—but he was grateful for the long good-bye, to tell those he loved what he thought of them.

"Which brings me to you," he said. Then he was quiet. He rocked the porch swing while I looked out to the yard and pond. Michael beat cancer once, fair and square. But it did a U-turn. Why Michael instead of a guy like me? "Bugs me how fair it ain't," I told him.

Michael handed me a copy of the North Georgia News. "Pretty good article today by another Watkins fella," he said. "I think it's going to tick off our football coach, but I'd wager what's in print is what Coach Lawler said about his starting quarterback. The kid can write, Ron."

"'Cept to his father," I told him. I read the first few lines of the article, then tossed it beside Michael on the swing.

"What happened to those Civil War letters you've got that you gave me copies of?" he asked.

"The ones my father read obsessively? Still got 'em. Why?"

"Writing's in your family is all," Michael said. "You think Wes would want those?"

I didn't know. I just knew you didn't want to ask for them, or for anything, from me.

"You could offer to send them to him, as an olive branch, and send him some personal letters. He'll read yours when he's ready to hear your story," Michael said. "I wrote some letters to a soldier's mom. Damon Maxwell—he drove the Humvee in our convoy when we got ambushed by the insurgents. Actually, the IED explosion was first. Then came the firefight. The blast killed him. It should have killed me, but his side of the vehicle absorbed most of the blast and almost all of the shrapnel. His body took the blows meant for me. I checked his vitals before charging into the building where we were being shot at. If he'd had any heartbeat at all, I would have stayed with him. Probably died too on that street instead of almost bleeding out in a room staring down a terrorist."

I asked if Mrs. Maxwell ever wrote back.

"Once," he admitted. "I'd tried to see her, which was a

bad idea. She shut the door in my face. I wrote to apologize—it was a surprise visit, seeing as she blocked my calls. She wrote back, thanking me for telling her the truth, but saying that she couldn't forgive me yet."

I asked him what he had hoped to get out of writing those letters.

He didn't know. "Most of the time, I think she's right. If I had just been more careful. But they'd never tried an attack like that. We thought they were concentrated somewhere else—somewhere we were heading, a mosque where artillery rounds were being lobbed at our base. We were fooled. I failed Damon and the rest of my company. It was my fault is what it boils down to. I guess I wrote to Damon's mom because his memory will never fade, and although she won't let me, if the opportunity ever presented itself, I would help her and her family."

"But like you said, it never presented itself."

"Just because you don't get the response you want, or none at all, it doesn't mean you haven't planted a seed. As long as you do it not expecting to get back, I think you'll be fine. You're doing it because it's the right thing, because in your walk with God, he's asking it of you, as a reminder if nothing else. A humbler."

"Mrs. Maxwell know you've got cancer?"

"Probably not," Michael said. "I'll have to write her a final one soon. Not sure what I'll say. Just bless her, tell her I will pray for her. That I'll be happy to see her son again. Mainly, I hope the bitterness that's inside of her gets let out. If it has to come at my passing, so be it. It'd be better for her if it came sooner, or separate from it, but if that's not in her plan, I can't do anything about it. Except pray."

Michael picked up the newspaper and handed it to me. "Write to Wes, and think about mentioning those letters. Our time isn't God's time. I think he's more concerned with the effort and heart we put into it, that's where the fruit comes from. He works in his own ways, and when he fulfills his plan, it's always better than what we envisioned. Don't stop writing, hoping, till your ticker stops ticking."

So that's what I'm doing. Continuing to write and hoping that one day you'll see fit to maybe, just maybe, forgive me for all the things I wasn't.

Chapter 48

When the doorbell rang and Emmy opened her apartment door, there stood Wes, one hand gripping a bouquet of tulips, the other a roll of packing tape.

"Hey," he said. "I promised I'd help you pack boxes."

Emmy held the door. Its edges felt heavy in her grip. She could close it, and with that, close the book on her relationship with Wes. Perhaps they'd be friends, a year from now, when she returned.

She studied his solemn features. No, they couldn't be friends. That would hurt too much. This was the only man she'd seriously considered marrying. To go from that to buddies? Impossible. In sitcoms, maybe, but not here.

So there it was. Give him a chance, or shut him out for good. Emmy gripped the side of the door, trying to decide.

In the hallway, Baxter howled. She heard him charge the door. He brushed past her and jumped up on Wes, who stumbled back two steps before regaining his footing.

Emmy laughed. "Baxter says yes, so come on in."

Wes put the bouquet in the sink and set the packing tape on the counter.

"You are such a guy," Emmy said. "You brought me flowers on moving day. I've already packed vases."

"Then how about a plastic cup?"

She pointed to the cabinet, and Wes arranged the tulips.

"Beautiful!" Emmy said.

Wes put his hands on his hips as if in triumph. "I've come a long way from the brown belt, black shoes man you first met, huh?"

Emmy didn't say anything, and Wes sprung into action. "Enough talk. Let's get this apartment into shape. Do you want me to call someone for the big stuff—bed, TV, couch?"

"Why, you can't handle lifting one end?"

Wes smiled. "It's on."

Once the furniture was out, they developed a system pretty quick: Emmy packed; Wes transported to the U-Haul in the parking lot. While she worked in her bedroom closet, he stayed respectfully outside the bedroom door.

Halfway through the closet, Emmy began to worry that Wes had overworked himself and asked him to make a lunch run. He checked his blood sugar levels and said he'd be fine but did as he was told. While he was away, Emmy surveyed the remainder of the closet. Wes hadn't said anything, but surely when he entered her apartment, he understood that only family photos remained out, waiting to be packed. His part in her life was boxed up first. She'd done it the night before.

He came back with sandwiches and bottled waters. They sat on the floor and ate, mostly in silence. Emmy half expected a speech from Wes, but she didn't get one. It was almost as if the help was out of penance. Baxter trotted over and sat beside Wes.

When they finished lunch, all that remained was the boxes from the closet. Emmy knew she couldn't avoid it but still prolonged the inevitable. She handed him boxes of clothes and shoes, and he dutifully carried them down to the U-Haul. She took the two boxes with his name marked clearly on top and put them in the empty living room.

"I just thought they'd be better if you kept them," she said. "I don't want you to think—"

"Look, I understand," he said. "I'm not mad." He picked up the boxes and walked out toward his car.

Emmy listened to his footsteps echo in the stairwell. She waited by the kitchen counter, trying to think of what to say. What to feel.

Wes returned. He stood in the doorway, and as if on cue, Baxter ran to him. Wes bent down to pet his head. "About us . . ."

"I wasn't ready," Emmy said.

"I know. I rushed you. I was on a roll though. Freelance was going well, I was starting graduate school, getting to know my dad, and my mom was fine, even happy. So I figured, hey, life is good, why not propose?"

"It wasn't that I didn't want to say yes."

"The timing, I get it. Our timing was off. But there's something else too. I was basing our relationship and you off the . . . discoveries in my parents' lives. Everyone was coming at me. And I had to get ahead of the curve, know something before I was told so I wouldn't be shocked. I was tired of reacting. So the pieces to your story—it got in my head. I needed to find out about you, and him."

"I should have told you earlier. I know I need to close that chapter; I just don't know how."

Wes shook his head. "All this stuff is the same, isn't it? Me and my parents. You and what happened to Gabe. Running off and trying to juggle your life with your problems and not asking for help—it's disastrous. For me anyway. I should have talked about my concerns and told you where my head was—or wasn't. I lost my mind, and I think I lost you in the process."

"Wes—"

"I convinced myself we were at a crossroads and I was going to find out about you and us. I guess I did—more about me than you—how undeserving I was of you."

"Wes, I'm leaving tomorrow—" Emmy pleaded. "Can we talk about this—"

"When you get back? I can't wait, Emmy. I think our biggest problem has been not totally opening up. Instead of thinking about getting on one knee in Roswell or when you returned from your training, I should have sat on a bench with you and told you how I was feeling. I would have wanted to know about Gabe too—all of it. What happened doesn't change how I feel about you. There's this mirror you're looking in, and you hate the reflection because of a memory of what you were like a long time ago. It's a smudge that won't go away, but it's not who you are anymore. God's done a lot with you since that night. Think about it, Emmy—how many lives have you saved? How many people have you given a second chance? But you won't give one to yourself. How long is that going to drive you? You're going off to war, but I almost wonder if it's a relief to you, that you've got more scars and wounds stateside than over there. You're not being fair to yourself."

Emmy sat on the floor.

"You deserve to hear this from somebody better than me," Wes said. "Maybe it would resonate better. I heard the same things from my father about my mother, and I couldn't get it into my thick skull. Who was he to say those things? How could he talk about forgiveness after what he did? He was the perfect example though. He released himself of those sins and knew he couldn't change the course they created. But here and now, he could live a life worth feeling pretty good about. He rebounded. You could too, Emmy. Don't let it suck the life out of you. It's bad enough that I lost you over my own mistakes. I don't want to see you continue to lose yourself over regrets."

Chapter 49

Wes bobbed his head and stood on tiptoes to peer over the crowd of well-wishers who had gathered for this send-off. Through the flags and balloons, he spotted Emmy in the formation.

As one, the unit pivoted to face the Canton downtown courthouse and the noted dignitaries. Their boots echoed in unison as they came to parade rest. The company commander, the Georgia National Guard commander, the Canton mayor, and even the governor would send them off after a handful of speeches. The music and crowd noise died down so people could listen to the speakers. Wes took that at his cue and turned to walk up the street away from the courthouse.

Walking step by step with him was Lynn Gavin. "Did you see her?" she asked, a grin on her face.

"Yep," Wes said. "She's near the center of the formation."

"Wonderful," Lynn said. "Well, everyone is waiting for us. Shall we?"

Wes and Lynn walked to their gathered friends. Addy welcomed them at the corner of the street, waving her arms. With her were Emmy's parents, Paul and Betty Gavin, about a dozen nurses and hospital colleagues, and two teenagers off to the side—one in a wheelchair. The other held her hand.

Whether Keith Starks had been after a story about Mandy and not Nate, Wes didn't really care. He'd let Mandy know that when she got a chance, he'd like to talk to her about her recovery, for the paper of course. Then during the brief interview and off-topic conversation with Mandy, he mentioned a nurse who'd treated Nate and had given her parents directions to Emory after the crash, and, wouldn't you know it, she would be deploying soon and it'd be wonderful if people would come out and show their support to her unit at the farewell. So she found a ride with a friend, and Nate, still weak from his hospital stay but eager to see Emmy off, showed up too.

"Emmy's going to love this," Lynn said.

Would she? Wes wondered. He'd said his piece, poured out his heart, but where it left them, he didn't know. He was out of words, and Emmy hadn't really had any to begin with. But Wes knew he'd needed to say those things, and he felt deep down Emmy needed to hear them. She needed to know she was loved in every way possible. Whether it got them back to firm footing was irrelevant.

"Here's the leash," Paul said, eager to hand over Baxter. It was Emmy's one consolation, to give Wes the responsibility of taking care of him. She'd shown up at his house in the morning with Baxter and all his things. A small thing but significant at the same time, and it wasn't lost on Wes.

Once the speeches were over, music blared from loudspeakers near the courthouse, and the crowd roused itself into cheers. Wes's contingent did their share of waving and screaming. Wes found himself tapping his feet nervously like a kid waiting for recess. He shifted his footing and raised and lowered his head to try and see Emmy within the company ranks.

"That's a good thing you did there," Lynn said.

"I'd like to think I can sometimes get it right. Her dad's not going to be happy when he finds out they met, but he'll have to deal with it." "I'm handling Mandy's rehab work too," Lynn said. "I'll try and smooth things over."

"There she is!" Addy screamed. The soldiers marched in formation. The block of gathered supporters raised their cheering up a notch. Emmy was looking straight ahead, and Wes could practically read her mind. She probably thought the people on the streets were for other soldiers. On her first deployment, she'd left friendships and family behind in Athens. If Wes could give her one gift before she left, it would be the assurance that if she wanted it, Talking Creek could be her home.

"On three," Addy urged the group. "One . . . two . . . three—Emmy, we love you!"

Emmy turned and saw the family and friends, signs, balloons, and flags, all there for her. She spotted Nate and Mandy and put a hand to her mouth in surprise. Then she beamed from ear to ear and waved, which set off the entire street, as the rest of the nearby crowd recognized who this large group was screaming at.

The company's march was formal, but not overly so. Some family members hopped the lines to give a husband or wife or brother or sister one last hug. Emmy pointed at Wes, as if singling out an instigator. Wes shrugged and feigned innocence.

Then Emmy pointed at him again, made a signal for him to approach the line. He ran to catch up and leaned in as if Emmy was going to give him a quick message. Without missing a step, Emmy reached both hands behind Wes's neck, pulled him in and planted a kiss on his lips.

"Keep the ring around, okay?" she said, looking him in the eye. Wes nodded. She released her arms and kept marching.

Wes stood in the middle of the street as the column marched off to war.

Chapter 50

"Explain to me again why I've got to wear these?" Ron asked.

"They're khakis and a dress shirt," Wes said.

"I can see that."

"They're nice."

"But not comfortable," Ron said. "It's got to be, what, ninety degrees outside? May weather and khakis don't mix for me."

"Sorry," Wes said. "We're going to cure you of your aversion to buttoned-up shirts before you walk out of here. I've got the keys, and I'm not letting you in my car unless you pass the dress code."

Ron eyed his son. "Fine," he said, grabbing the folded dress shirt from the table. "It's your mom you get your stubbornness from."

Dressed and released, Ron hopped into Wes's Camry. "Sure appreciate the ride," he said when they hit the road. "And the couch at your place. I'll call the utilities for my apartment as soon we get there so I'll be out of your hair."

"Don't worry about it," Wes said. "You hungry?"

"I could eat a horse."

"Don't think that's legal in Georgia. But I know a place with burgers and salads once we get into town."

"That'll do."

At Reese's Café, the owner, Milton Reese, had retired a year ago, but his oldest son kept up the tradition of greeting each customer from a rocking chair outside the door like a bouncer at a bar. Once Wes and Ron passed the eyeball test, he gave them the standard greeting. "Boys," he said with a nod.

"I'd tip my cap to ya, but my son here wanted me dressed prim and proper."

Reese Jr. chuckled. "Specials list is on the tables. Hope you enjoy."

When they entered the café, Ron froze. "You are one conniving son of a gun," he said. Janet was waiting for them in a corner booth.

"Get it from my father," Wes said.

Janet rose and gave Wes a hug. She then looked at Ron, who hadn't moved a step since spotting her. "Well, aren't you going to sit down?"

Ron shuffled to the booth. "I'll sit as far away as you want me to. It's no trouble," he said. "This was nice of Wes, but really, I understand. I know how hard this must be for you. It's hard for me, honestly, and I'm the dirt bag. In fact, these clothes Wes picked out are hindering my ability not to be nervous. You just say the word and I'll step out and you and your son can have a nice meal together."

"She wanted to see you," Wes said.

"You did?"

She nodded. "I'm kind of surprised too," she said. "But I have a favor to ask."

"Sure," Ron said. "Seems like 'I owe you one' doesn't really cut it though, huh?"

"It might," she said.

Wes could see Ron waiting for an answer, and Janet seemed to hold it on the tip of her tongue for as long as she could bear. "A few months ago you came to my physician's office asking if you could see about donating a kidney to me. Well, do you still want to?"

Chapter 51

Emmy grabbed her medic bag and slid off the Blackhawk floor, landing with both feet on the concrete tarmac. She ducked her head and felt the rush of wind from the chopper blades as she and a squad of soldiers walked back to the operating base for a debriefing. It'd been a successful mission—no casualties and enough reliable intel from the locals to know where the Taliban was trying to make inroads.

In the debriefing room, Emmy took her helmet off and picked a spot in the back. The platoon commander, a scrappy lieutenant from the Citadel, fired off his report. *He's a fast-track officer,* Emmy thought, *bent on results and bent even more on pinning the Taliban in their caves and across the Afghani border.* She was fully aware that their increased presence had led to her short-fuse deployment, so she certainly didn't mind if soldiers like this one took the fight to them. That he was an excellent planner and hadn't gotten his platoon boxed into a canyon or kill box and thus avoided a need for Emmy's services was that much the better.

The group dismissed, Emmy tucked her helmet under her arm and headed for the barracks—wooden frames and serviceable toilets and bathrooms with hot water running, most of the time. The engineers from the Guard unit that had built them had done a solid job.

Emmy shared a room with two other women. Although outnumbered by men in almost every facet of the military, there were perks for the females—such as the pick of the rooms and their own section in the bathrooms. She tossed her gear on top of her bed and reached under it to pull out her laptop.

It still boggled her mind that within the span of a few minutes she could go from treating a bullet wound to checking her e-mail or looking at what her friends were doing on Facebook. The Internet service wasn't always reliable, but it worked enough of the time.

"Anything from Wes?" asked her roommate. She was resting on the top bunk adjacent to Emmy's bottom bunk with one eye on a paperback and the other on Emmy.

Emmy smiled. "About to see," she said. "Yep. He's on a roll."

Colleen rolled her eyes. "Has he missed a day?" she asked. "Next e-mail you send out, tell him I'd like some candy corn in your next care package."

"Will do," Emmy said.

It had become a regular routine—finishing a shift or completing a mission to return to his words and life back in Talking Creek. She was able to filter her thoughts into e-mails or over Skype conversations, and it helped pass the time and get a grasp on the stress and rigors of being deployed. Sometimes she wondered how'd she done it in Iraq with no one to write home to besides her parents and a friend from nursing school. Wes had set up a Groups page on Facebook, and she was able to see the well-wishes, even reconnect with a few friends from Athens.

She and Wes had actually grown closer during the deployment, and she was glad. He'd confided in her as his parents went through tests. In September Ron had been cleared by the doctors to donate a kidney. Wes and his dad were spending a decent amount of time together and enjoying it, a welcome change for him.

In October, Emmy had lamented with Wes a Georgia loss to LSU in overtime and cheered a ten-point win in Jacksonville against Florida. Wes sent her the DVD replays in his weekly care packages.

They'd both grown in their faith since she'd arrived in Afghanistan. Wes was more open, going to church, asking for prayers at church and on Facebook. Emmy was accepting the prayers and support family and friends offered instead of keeping everyone at arm's length.

Wes's e-mail addressed the upcoming transplant, slated in two days—a week before Thanksgiving—in Nashville. Emmy was reading through his thoughts slowly, so she could respond with prayers and encouragement, when she heard the boots running toward her room.

"Stewart, a bird's carrying casualties, ETA five minutes," called a fellow medic.

With those casualties and another rushed mission, Emmy wouldn't return to her room until after the transplant had taken place.

Chapter 52

Ron put one hand on the bed railing and braced himself for the all-important task of remote retrieving. But a hand reached out and grabbed the remote for him.

Wes thumbed the on button. "Easy, bud. You had a kidney plucked out of you yesterday, I'll get it. Dawgs, right? Need anything else?"

"Something to drink. Kinda nice to be staying at such a swanky joint on someone else's dime," Ron said.

"The least they could do," Wes replied, handing him an orange juice. "As long as you don't wear out your welcome with the nurses, you'll be fine."

"Well, you don't need to stay up here with me and your mom," Ron said. "Head back down to Talking Creek whenever you're ready. I'll call Otis and the fellas to help out. Call in a few favors."

"Hey, I'm your son. It's my job," Wes said. "I'm happy to do it," he added. "Be back in a few minutes. I'm going to get a sandwich from the cafeteria."

A year ago Ron wouldn't have believed it—sitting with Wes, talking, and watching a football game. He had imagined it so many times, telling Wes that he was sorry and wished he'd done better. He'd even occasionally told his imaginary son that he'd sober up, get his act together, and come sweeping in as father of the year. It never happened, and for so long there was the all-enveloping shame, until he did get his act together, with the help of friends.

Help. Friends. Otis, Michael, and the rest. They'd pulled him out of his personal hell, and he held on to them when they started their various dips and wanes. The battles never totally left them, but—

"What's the score?" Wes said, sandwich and a bottle of water in hand.

Ron didn't answer right away. "Never thought I'd see the day," he finally said.

"What, that I'd eat healthy?" Wes asked, taking a bite out of his turkey sandwich.

"That you'd let me in."

"Well, I didn't admit you here; the hospital staff did," Wes said, grinning.

"That not what I—"

"I know what you meant," Wes said. He set his plate down and put a hand on his father's shoulder. "Promise me one thing."

"Anything."

"No more apologies."

Wes returned to his sandwich, and the two Watkins boys watched a quarter of Dawgs football together. They talked about the ref's horrible holding penalty and how the new running back from La Grange was handling blitz pickups. They argued over whether Sanford stadium was a loud venue. They lamented years when the Dawgs let championships slip away, right down to the turnover that lost a game.

The camera flashed to the crowd, and Ron watched as it panned through the families, college kids, and couples. "Would have been fun to have three generations there—you, me, and your grandpa."

"Still a chance for three generations," Wes said. "One of these days I'll get married; my luck's just been a little bad getting around to the question."

"And I haven't met her yet," Ron said.

"She'll be coming back home in a month, if all goes well. They get a week in the States before going back and finishing out their deployment. You'll meet her then."

"I'll hold you to that."

Wes smiled. "Want to see the ring?"

Ron wiped a bead of sweat from his forehead. "Mind turning up the AC a little bit while you're at it? Getting a little bit sweaty."

Wes adjusted the AC, then went digging in his overnight bag. Ron fanned his shirt and tilted his head to receive the first gush of cool air from the vent above the bed. He closed his eyes and thought of his father's favorite place in their house—the front porch. His father had always enjoyed a beverage and the breeze of the overhead fan after a long day at work or in the yard on the weekend. Ron would join him sometimes, with a glass of fresh lemonade, his smallish legs swinging back and forth on the rocking chair. It was on that porch where Ron's dad was at his best—teaching his son the intricacies of tree climbing, fort building, and throwing a baseball. Ron wished he could have trapped his dad like a firefly, kept him on the shelf. Then whenever the distant, gambling-addict daddy entered the house, Ron could have run to his room, grab the mason jar sitting next to his toy soldiers, and popped open the daddy he loved to be around.

He felt a small pinch along his left arm and shifted his position, his eyes still closed. *Can't bottle the good without scooping up the bad as well,* he reminded himself. *What would Wes bottle of me?* he wondered. As precious few fond memories Ron had of his own father, there were even fewer available for his son. But he suppressed his guilt over Wes and his regret for his father's bare legacy. *I'm past that,* he reminded himself.

God had taken what little Ron had done and glued it together and brought him back to his family. It was the great repair job that only an appliance repairman could truly appreciate. All that appeared lost wasn't. He breathed in a deep breath of it, the cool reassurance of God's grace, and thanked the Lord, blessing by blessing, for his father, his son, and a renewed purpose.

When Ron opened his eyes, his son stood over him. A man now, with a ring destined for the finger of a lovely woman. Ron beamed with pride. "May I hold it?"

But the darnedest thing happened. He couldn't grip the box. After a few seconds, the pinch returned, this time stronger, wrapping his entire left arm. It raged into a shooting pain straight through his body and into his heart. He dropped the ring box and clutched his chest.

Just like Daddy, he thought. He knew his time was near. His vision blurred and turned white, but he managed a few more glimpses of his boy. The white circling his eyes dimmed Wes's panicked expression and bumbling with the call button to the nurses' station. Ron knew, even in the belly of a hospital, they couldn't save him. The pain actually eased then, when it became all-encompassing.

All that was left was Ron's love. He was ready. He took one last, long look at his son, and then his sight faded.

Chapter 53

Janet opened her eyes. She knew not to move—a day and an afternoon following the transplant, her belly felt like a sewn-up pillow. Slowly, she swiveled her head to see that her brother, Cory; sister, Glenda; and Wes were in the room. Glenda sat in the nearest chair, her hand on top of Janet's, rubbing it gently.

"So this is what a kidney transplant feels like," Janet said.

Glenda smiled. "Hurts, don't it?"

Despite the stitches, IV and catheter lines, and pain medication, Janet grinned. She couldn't help it. She'd gotten her body back with a new working part. She knew the transplant wasn't foolproof, but what a miracle of science, a physician carving an organ out of one human being to sustain life in another, and Janet gave thanks for that.

More than anything, Janet recognized God's plans in the events leading up to her transplant. She'd moved to Nashville to be closer to family but had received the benefit of some of the best health care facilities in the country. Had Wes not reconnected with Ron, she may not have had a donor for quite a while, if at all. Had Wes not forgiven her for her past, would she have been so open to Ron's gift? What if Paul Gavin had never visited? The wonderment of God began on those unseen paths. It was impossible to anticipate, to expect where his grace would come from and who would be traveling with it.

Janet looked at her son. "Looks like you need to get some sleep, Wes," she said. He had to be tired, commuting from one room and one parent to another. "Why don't you have Glenda drive you back to my place and take a nap? There are fresh sheets in the bedroom and a pantry full of snacks."

At first the only sound in the room came from the chirping on the monitors. Then Wes buried his head in his hands. Glenda leaned in toward Janet. "Honey, why don't you be the one to take a nap, and we can talk about this later."

"Talk about what?" Janet said, her voice rising. "What's wrong?" It felt like something bit her in her belly, and she flinched at the pain.

"Easy now," Glenda said.

Janet shook her head. "I want someone to tell me what's going on."

"He's gone," Wes said. "Ron's gone."

"How is that possible?" Janet demanded. "Kidney transplants—that just doesn't happen."

"Heart attack," Wes said. "Not the transplant. He had a heart attack a couple of hours ago—like his dad. He wasn't thorough in his medical history, so the doctors probably didn't know of the condition when they screened him and wouldn't have been looking for it. Dad didn't make it. He's gone, Mom."

Chapter 54

Wes looked up and down the control panel of the F-250 to find the heat controls to counter the snowy January landscape. He adjusted his seat and gripped the plush steering wheel, trying to work his hands into a sort of muscle memory of it, but no matter what he did, the driver's side felt empty, like he was just taking up space until the owner showed up to reclaim the keys.

A knock came on the passenger-side door, and Otis waved and hopped into the double cab.

"It's a little higher up than the Camry," Wes said.

"*I'm* higher up than the Camry," Otis said. "And I'm five foot eight."

Wes turned the ignition, and the F-250's engine roared. His F-250, given to him in Ron's will. "Takes some getting used to, all that muscle under the hood."

"I bet that's right, sedan man," Otis said.

They drove in silence, not because there was nothing to say but more that silence was the considerate choice for where they were headed. An hour and a half up the interstate, to Georgia 400 toward the mountains, and then they pulled onto a gravel road in Dahlonega. The gravel road elevated until they crested a hill that came out onto an open field with a large house tucked back toward the tree line. They hit a concrete carport and pulled off to the side.

An elderly woman came out of the house. "It's in the barn," she said.

They followed her, boots crunching the snow, to a barn behind the house. On the door there was a lock, and the woman fumbled through her pockets for the key. "Never in a million years thought I'd get a taker from the classified I put in the Atlanta paper," she said.

"I'm just as surprised as you are," Wes said. Otis's gloved hand squeezed his shoulder.

The first thing they saw in the barn was a large green tractor with a fresh coat of paint and immaculate tires. Every part of the tractor looked cared for and well maintained.

"Shane would take it out once a week," the woman told them. "Did his yard work himself. Got to be more difficult the older we got. We'd buy a couple cows and fatten them up and sell them off, so he'd let them take care of part of the yard. Was about ten years ago he started getting into his other hobby."

Wes walked past the tractor. Behind it, he found what he'd been looking for—what his dad had been looking for. "A 1970 F-100."

"That's what our pastor told me," the woman said. "I had him come out and help me with some things, including the classifieds for the cars. We were doing fine before the recession, but now I really don't know. I think I'll need all the help I can get to stay retired here. The Cadillac and little sports car went fast. I thought I'd have to give this one to the junkyard and sell it for parts."

Wes touched the F-100's hood. The paint was chipped and faded. He noticed a handful of dents, saw the wear in the cabin. The air in all the tires was low, the bumper in the back hung like a thread.

"Funny thing with this," the woman went on, "my husband bought it from a dealer in Ellijay to use it for toting wood and shovels and what-not around our property. Wasn't in the most pristine condition even then. It had probably been around the entire state in used-car lots before Elli-jay. He rode it pretty hard, as you can see. Then one day, he was fiddling around with it and came in and said he didn't have the heart to use the F-100 anymore. He'd rather just keep it around."

"Did he say why?" Wes asked.

"Found a picture in the glove compartment underneath the paperwork.

Guess he hadn't looked too hard in there before. Still there if you want to see it."

Wes opened the door to the passenger side and breathed in the old, musty smell. What memories it would have jogged for his dad! He sat inside and thumbed through the glove compartment and found the picture. The sides were worn, but the scene was unmistakable—Allatoona. "Unbelievable," he said. "All this time."

Ron and Janet stood in front of the huge railroad cut, Wes fidgeting in Ron's arms. They had the look of young parents—Janet's eyes urging whoever took the photograph to hurry or else they might lose Wes's attention, Ron stoic because he didn't want to be the one to mess up the shot.

Wes flipped it over and saw that Ron had written a small note.

> To whom it may concern,
>   I would like you to know that this truck was a blessing, and I hope it keeps on that way. It brought my father and me closer. And I'm sad to see it go and those memories gone with it, but please just take care of it for me. One day I plan on buying it back from you, and taking my boy for a ride. God willing, you'll be able to enjoy those kind of memories too.
> Sincerely,
> Ron

Wes drew a deep breath. "I'll trade you the F-250 for your truck."

"Son, you into drugs or something?"

Wes laughed. "No ma'am. This photo's been missing from a family album. This note was from my father. And all these years, he was right. I think he'd want to trade his new truck for his old one and call it even."

"Ain't nothing I'll take on an uneven field. Shane would have done the same."

"I can go to a car dealer and get cash for it and come back and make you an offer," Wes pleaded. "Please don't sell this to anyone else."

"Wes, you don't even know how to drive a stick," Otis said.

"I'll learn."

"You want to trade an F-250 for a beat-up clunker that you don't even know how to drive? It sure don't make any sense," the woman said. "But I seen what that note did to Shane before he passed. Made him think of his father. There's something about men and their fathers, connections, that make them pause and reflect. And this one's souring your financial skills."

"I'll write you a check," Wes said. "I don't have too much in savings . . ."

"How about this. If you're dead-set on trading me for something I'm not even going to drive, why don't we take both of these into town and you see if you can get a good deal on the F-250. And we'll use half the money to fix this thing up, and the other half to fix up some of my continued retirement."

Wes jumped out of the truck. "Deal!"

The woman shook her head as she shook Wes's hand. She turned to Otis. "He always like this?"

Otis smiled. "He gets it from his father."

Chapter 55

The bright Georgia sun penetrated the thick glass windows of Atlanta International's tunnel, forcing Emmy to shield her eyes and nearly collide with an ASO volunteer whose name tag said Rebecca.

"Anything I can help you with?" Rebecca asked.

"No, thank you," Emmy said. The airport had connecting flights to practically everywhere so the ASO group of volunteers was a large one, and Emmy wasn't completely surprised she'd been spotted so quickly. "Atlanta is my stop."

"Are you back on leave or done with your deployment?"

"Done, a month early. Didn't think I'd be home by April. They're shipping us back in waves."

Rebecca paused, like she wanted to say more. "Well, thank you for your service"—she looked down at Emmy's name patch on her carry-on bag— "Miss Stewart."

Outside the tunnel, she stopped to text Wes that she'd arrived. She was excited to see him, but nervous also. Her deployment had changed their relationship all for the better. They'd opened up to each other in letters and e-mails more than they had in person, but now that they'd be together each day, a question hung over their heads. Their relationship was no longer on pause. They'd have to move forward, or back.

She'd already moved forward once. On her weeklong leave in December, she could have returned to Athens and taken a dip into purgatory, knowing she'd miss the official anniversary. But she hadn't. She'd penned a letter and wished the Pattersons the best . . . and moved on. She'd pulled herself up from the bottom and tried to pull as many as she could from that pit as well. Admittedly she couldn't save everybody, but it wasn't a number she was after or trying to avoid, it was the act itself.

Another ASO volunteer approached her. Jenny, her name tag said. "Hello dear! So good to have you back in the States."

Emmy wanted to ask how Jenny knew she'd been deployed but thought Jenny was just making an educated guess. Out of the corner of her eye, she saw another ASO volunteer approach. "Amanda, won't you come over here?" Jenny called.

"You all are everywhere," Emmy said. "I came across your friend Rebecca just a second ago."

Jenny and Amanda studied Emmy with sparkling eyes, like they were dazzled by her presence.

"Is everything all right?" Emmy asked them.

"Oh . . . of course," Jenny said. "We're just so proud of our troops! Can we take your bag, buy you a coffee?"

"I'm fine, thanks. I've got a car waiting on me, so I'd better go." She heard them whispering as she left and heard her first name. She hadn't told them her name, had she?

The shuttle train whisked her from her terminal to the front of the airport, where the transportation and baggage areas were. The escalator to baggage claim was tall and massive, and she couldn't see beyond it. The effect led to anticipation for most returning soldiers native to Atlanta—they'd take the thirty-second escalator ride and come off to banners, babies, cousins, and loved ones holding signs, clapping, and jumping up and down. She'd seen it many times but never experienced it herself. Again, a product of her self-imposed estrangement.

But she was ready for that to change, to dig roots in a town like Talking Creek. "Five more minutes," she said. "Then I'm home free."

When she reached the top of the escalator, she watched a family in midembrace. A dad, a major, had returned, and he wrapped his burly arms around his two daughters, who giggled and smiled like it was their birthday. Within seconds they were joined by their mom and grandmothers, and pretty soon a big crowd enveloped them, to the delight of onlookers cheering the reunion. Emmy felt a ping of joy and a ping of regret at the same time.

She turned to head toward baggage claim when someone tapped her on the shoulder. "Emmy Stewart? I'm Joe, ASO volunteer. We've got a call for you. Can you follow me?"

Confused, Emmy followed Joe. His path led straight into the reunion crowd, and Emmy almost shouted to ask him why they didn't just go around, when the crowd parted. She took a few steps to follow him in and noticed that everyone had turned toward her. Voices hushed. Joe disappeared into the crowd.

Emmy moved carefully, as if walking in the dark. Why had so many ASO volunteers approached her? Why did Joe disappear so quickly? Why was everyone looking at her?

Suddenly, she knew. The anticipation, the wait, the fear of the unknown washed away as she realized a new chapter of her life was about to start.

And she wasn't afraid of it anymore.

She wasn't afraid to say yes, and in fact that would be the next word coming out of her mouth.

Because propped on one knee, in the middle of the crowd, Wes Watkins was waiting for her, with a smile as wide as a football field and a box as open as his heart, a sparkling diamond ring inside.

Also available from Graham Garrison

What makes a man a legend?

HERO'S TRIBUTE

A Novel

GRAHAM GARRISON

ISBN: 978-0-8254-2685-8